THE
SARDINE
DECEPTION

Leif Davidsen

THE SARDINE DECEPTION

Translated from the Danish by
Tiina Nunnally & Steve Murray

Fjord Press
Seattle
1986

For Ulla

Translation copyright © 1986 Fjord Press

Title of Danish edition: *Uhellige alliancer*
Copyright © 1984 Leif Davidsen
Originally published by Forlaget Vindrose, Copenhagen

Published and distributed by:
Fjord Press
P.O. Box 16501
Seattle, Washington 98116

Design & typography: Accent & Alphabet, Seattle
Cover design: Art Chantry Design, Seattle
Printing: Edwards Brothers, Inc.

Library of Congress Cataloging-in-Publication Data:

Davidsen, Leif, 1950–
  The sardine deception.

  Translation of: Uhellige alliancer.
  1. País Vasco (Spain) — History — Autonomy and independence
movements — Fiction. I. Title.
PT8176.14.A8U4413 1986   839.8'1374   86-2094
ISBN 0-940242-15-X (alk. paper)

Printed in the United States of America
First edition, April 1986

THE
SARDINE
DECEPTION

1

*E*veryone who has a TV knew my wife. That's why the whole affair surrounding her disappearance under mysterious circumstances received a great deal of attention in the press. I was married to Charlotte and played a significant role in her beautifully staged death, but, just like in our marriage, I was only a supporting actor. Who would be interested in some obscure jurist in the Ministry of Social Affairs? One of the great myths in our society is that every person has a story to tell, but only the weekly tabloids selling happiness take that myth seriously.

My unobtrusive role was nothing new. I was used to being introduced as Poul Jensen, married to the well-known TV journalist Charlotte Damsborg. Even my name invites anonymity. Charlotte used a stage name; I kept my own and lived decidedly in her shadow.

As a jurist, I think that there should be order to things. A chaotic life is only for the very young. Or for artists. Society only functions if we accept and obey democratically adopted laws. A marriage works on the same principles. There are certain rules and standards for interaction between people. If you follow them, everything goes more smoothly and calmly. I don't believe in great excesses. Wild gestures and a temperament that shifts from hot to cold are foreign to my nature, and to the study of law as well. I'm often accused of being old-fashioned. To that I say: A belief in order and regularity, in the necessity for continuity, isn't old-fashioned — it's plain common sense.

7

Charlotte was just the opposite, but we had arrived at a comfortable arrangement.

The affair surrounding her disappearance began in classic fashion with the visit of two police officers. Began for me, that is. The whole thing had started long before, of course. Two officers arrived. One middle-aged, the other young.

There's nothing wrong with my memory. The study of law demands nothing more than a sturdy seat of the pants and a good memory. I have both, and I passed with reasonable grades. The account of what happened is as I saw it. Nothing has been left out. Nothing has been added, within the limitations of the written word. None of us can escape a personal point of view, but I've tried to live up to the rule Charlotte followed as a journalist: tell the story straight, without beating around the bush, and be fair. Digressions belong to the realm of art, she used to say.

To get to the point.

They rang my doorbell around 9 o'clock on a cold February evening when the last snow still lay like excrement along the curb. The kids (we have two) were asleep, and I was smoking my pipe and reading. Peace had descended on the five-room apartment, insulated according to all the codes, where the temperature was the standard 20°C.

They stood knocking imaginary snow off their shoes when I opened the door.

"We're police officers. May we come in for a moment?" asked the older of the two.

"It's concerning your wife."

"Come in, come in. Let me take your coats."

They sat down on the sofa. Just on the edge. They said yes to my offer of a cup of coffee from the thermos and complimented me on the cozy living room, where order had been restored now that the kids were in bed. A few prints. Hardwood floor with a light-colored rug of pure wool. Framed pictures of friends, children, and the two of us.

The older man, who had introduced himself as Jørgensen, said, "I understand you're a bachelor for the time being?" He immediately looked ill-at-ease.

"That's right. My wife is on a leave of absence."

He hesitated, so I volunteered, "Charlotte is in Spain. She's collecting material for a book about the democratization of the country."

"Your wife has had an accident," said the younger man. And he continued with the same brutality on his face and in his voice: "She was in a bar this morning when a bomb exploded. I'm afraid she's dead."

The older one coughed, or rather cleared his throat, and fumbled for some matches. I recall that he had broad fingers and nails clipped short, as if bitten to the quick.

"We're very sorry," he said, lighting a cigarette. It sounded sincere enough to my ears, but what are you supposed to do? What do you say? Do you cry? Do you throw up your hands? Say that it can't be true? That there must be some mistake?

As I said, wild gestures just aren't my style. So I got up and went into the children's room. Stine and Jakob were asleep. Stine with her fingers in her mouth. She had spit out her pacifier. Jakob had kicked off the covers. They both smelled sweetly of milk and yogurt. I felt completely empty inside. Just thought stupidly: Now they don't have a mother anymore. And then I thought even more stupidly: Good thing it isn't me who's dead. After all, I'm the one who has taken care of the kids most of the time. Charlotte always travels so much. Traveled. Then I cried a little anyway, in the dimness of the children's room, before I went back into the living room.

Jørgensen sat drinking coffee, smoking yet another cigarette. The younger one stood looking at our/my books. I lit a cigarette

and took a gulp of cold coffee. Brushed imaginary crumbs off
the table and carefully put my bookmark in its place. Chaos is
held at bay by doing trivial things properly.

"What happened and where?"

Jørgensen leaned forward.

"We don't have all the details. This is Spain we're talking
about, you know. What we have is from the embassy down there
in Madrid. But it seems that your wife was unlucky enough to be
in a bar in San Sebastián — that's in northern Spain — when a
bomb went off. Apparently several people were killed. Even
more were injured. Nobody knows who planted the bomb.
Some group of extremists. It seems there are a lot of terrorists in
those parts."

"So she was in Basque country."

"You didn't know that?"

"Charlotte traveled around a lot. I got a letter every so often.
I got one a couple of days ago. We talked on the telephone, but
she is — was — a big girl who could take care of herself."

"When was the last time you talked to her?" It was the
younger one who asked. He was still very interested in the books
and spoke with his back half-turned to me.

"About a month ago. She wanted to know how the children
were." I didn't mention that I thought it had been a long time
and that I'd been both angry and worried. That I thought she
was really pushing it.

"From San Sebastián?" He pronounced it with flat a's.

"No . . . from Barcelona, I think."

There was silence for a moment.

"Where is her body?" I asked. The word had an ugly taste
to it.

"It's in San Sebastián. If you like, you can claim it yourself
or let the embassy take care of it." Now it was the older one
talking again.

"I'll go down there myself, of course."

"Mr. Jensen," said the younger man, "do you know exactly what your wife was doing in San Sebastián?"

"All I know is that she was working on a book about Spain. She probably needed some information and went to San Sebastián to talk with the Basques. They want autonomy, right? She was a journalist."

"How long had she been gone?"

"Almost three months."

"And she was coming back when?"

"She'd been given a six-month leave of absence. She said on the phone she might come home at any time."

The younger officer turned around. He stood there rocking back and forth on the balls of his feet.

"Why would someone want to blow up your wife?"

"I understood that she was just unlucky and happened to be in the bar when the bomb exploded."

"Yes, that's what we think too, but she was a journalist, after all, and journalists stick their noses into a lot of things. Some people might regard journalists as spies of some sort — wouldn't you agree?"

I didn't answer. He was still rocking on the balls of his feet.

"Mr. Jensen, did your wife mention in any of her letters or on the phone that she had established contact with any terrorist groups?"

"No."

"Does the name ETA mean anything to you?"

"Yes. It's the name of a Basque terrorist group — partisans, I think they call themselves. They want autonomy for the Basques, or probably would rather have their own country. Something like the Palestinians."

"That's right. You seem to know about these things."

"I read the papers."

"Then I'll ask you in another way. Was your wife in contact with the ETA?"

"Not that I know of. It's possible that she tried to get an interview with them. How should I know?"

"Your wife sympathized with the ETA, didn't she?"

I was feeling bad and now I got angry.

"My wife always tried to be objective. And I don't know what the hell it is you're trying to imply. But if you're implying that my wife was sympathetic to terrorists, then you're walking on thin ice. You come here and tell me my wife is dead — and then the next minute you're intimating that she sympathized with murderers. Where the hell do you get off?"

"Now, now, Mr. Jensen. We're not intimating anything," said the older officer, who was sitting down. "We just want to be sure that the bomb wasn't intended for your wife."

"You mean you aren't sure of that?"

The expression on his face could be read either way.

"Let's put it another way," said the younger one. "Did your wife, to your knowledge, have connections that were other than professional with terrorist groups?"

I gave the older officer an entreating look.

"I don't know what you mean. My wife was an independent person."

"That's obvious." The younger officer was now looking directly at me.

"What the hell do you mean?"

"You can't call abandoning her husband and children for months at a time completely normal."

"Your reactionary views on sex roles don't interest me, and as a matter of fact I don't feel like listening to you anymore."

"Come now," said the older one. "It wasn't meant that way. You look like an even-tempered man. But it's clear that you're upset, and we won't bother you any longer . . ." He took a note-pad out of his pocket and wrote his name with square letters: A. Jørgensen. And a telephone number. Underneath he wrote another name, P. Simonsen, and a seven-digit number.

"That's the number of the Danish embassy in Madrid and our contact man. If there's anything we can do for you, don't hesitate to call."

"Thanks."

"And as for the press . . ."

"The press?"

"Yes. Your wife was a well-known personality, you know, so her death will probably be covered extensively tomorrow — in certain papers, at any rate."

"You mean that *Ekstra Bladet* and *B.T.* will scrap the front page for this?"

"Something like that."

"Can't you keep her name out of it? What about her mother?"

"I'm sorry. That's impossible. We have freedom of the press in Denmark, you know, and your wife's mother was informed just about the same time you were. We can keep it quiet for a couple of hours, maybe until tomorrow."

I thanked him, and with a "don't mention it" he got up and signaled to his colleague. They went out in the hallway and found their own coats. Only Jørgensen shook my hand.

"Once again, Mr. Jensen, I'm very sorry, and have a good trip to Spain, though that may sound strange. And remember, if there's anything we can help you with, give us a ring."

"I'll do that."

Then they left.

I had just turned off the light in the hall, looked in on the children, got a beer out of the refrigerator and sat down, when the telephone rang. The predators were already on the scent.

2

*I*t was an SAS flight departing at 11 o'clock from Copenhagen airport, non-stop for Madrid. Several things happened before I got that far.

The first reporter to phone was from *Ekstra Bladet*. I got rid of him by saying he could come over in an hour with a photographer. He'd get an exclusive on the story. You learned a thing or two by living with a journalist. He mentioned a deadline but seemed satisfied all the same. How had they gotten Charlotte's name already? So much for Mr. Jørgensen's promise.

After that I called Helle, one of Charlotte's colleagues at the radio station — one of Denmark's influential women. She was shocked, of course, but kept her head.

I got the sleeping kids into some clothes. Checked to see that the lights were turned off, the cups rinsed, the locks fastened — little things — and carried the sleeping children out to Helle's warm, waiting car.

"Did you pack a suitcase for yourself and one for the kids?" Yes, I did.

We drove off just as the press showed up. They didn't see us.

Helle's husband, Henrik, had coffee ready. And he had brought up a bed from the basement that we tucked the sleeping children into. They would have to be told in the morning. Stine probably wouldn't understand it, but Jakob already understood a great deal at four and a half.

I called Charlotte's mother from the large, hospitable house in Gentofte. She was asleep, the woman from next door said with a slightly lilting Lolland accent. The doctor had been there.

She was in good hands. Yes, it was terrible what had happened.
Disgusting! The violence in the world today! I hung up.

We talked about practical things. Did I have any money?
Some. And Eurochecks on our joint account. My ticket? Helle
would take care of that. She would get the radio station's travel
agency to handle it—then I wouldn't have to pay cash either. A
practical woman. We drank whiskey, poured with a liberal hand.

"The children can stay here, of course," said Helle. "No
problem. They like us and we like them, and they get along well
with our own kids."

I thanked her. And she said, "Oh, don't be so stuffy, Poul."

Once, a long time ago, I was a little in love with her, in spite
of myself perhaps. Still remembered the way her soft body had
pressed against mine at a party. But I was monogamous, both on
principle and by nature. Eight years of marriage and only a
couple of affairs. Both one-night stands and nothing to write
home about.

Later in the evening she asked me, "How was your relationship, toward the end? Would you have stayed together?"

You can't escape it these days. Wherever the young middle
class gathers, they discuss marriage, relationships, sex roles.
You're supposed to bare your soul and explain how you manage
to cope with that difficult task: living together.

I answered, "You know how Charlotte was."

"That's no answer."

"What do you want me to say?"

"What was your relationship like?"

"We had reached a comfortable arrangement. We were different, but we'd found a way of living together that satisfied both
of us. There's nothing more to say about it now, is there?"

"You're avoiding the issue," she said amid a haze of cigarette
smoke.

She was probably right. I sat in the airplane, eating cardboard food and drinking passable red wine. What was our relationship like for the past eight years, legally married for the last four? It was an appropriate time to take stock, I thought.

We had our ups and downs, like everyone else. I *was* avoiding the issue. I already missed the kids. Their soft arms around my neck. Unlike everyone else in my circle of friends, I really don't like to travel. I have the impression that that's almost as great a crime as being monogamous. The world is safer at home than abroad.

In the morning I had told the children that their mother was dead. They didn't understand. "Is she coming home soon?" Jakob had asked. She's always traveling. I explained gently that Mommy was dead. That she would never come home again.

People normally don't talk about death, even though we see traffic accidents all the time. We get rid of death just like we get rid of the garbage. We burn it.

The children cried like they were supposed to, but I don't think they understood much. Who knows? Helle stood in the doorway in a thin blouse and underpants. "I'll talk to them later," she said, taking three long strides and gathering them up in her arms.

"Come on! Breakfast is ready."

I sat in the airplane, zooming south over a snow-speckled Europe; I tried to think about Charlotte. We had met each other because of Spain — in a Spanish course at the Folkeuniversitet, an advanced class. I fell for her like a ton of bricks, and miraculously enough she fell for me. And in a few weeks we were living together. As we had been ever since, more or less.

Sexual faithfulness isn't very fashionable in our circle, to put it mildly. We of the new middle class often regard jealousy like a nun regards a sailor's bulge, if you'll pardon the expression. Yet time after time, jealousy hits us hard, right in the gut. But our blind faith in the power of words and conversation makes it seem like a minor problem that we can talk ourselves out of, or so we stubbornly insist. And yet we're often just as jealous as everyone else.

I'm willing to admit it. To use a banal expression, Charlotte was unfaithful to me. Not often, but regularly just the same, and frequently with men she actually despised. Male chauvinists, "sexual fascists," as she called those lucky fellows. When she wasn't going to bed with them, that is. She never wanted to live with them. She preferred a man like me — loving, tender, aware, a man who loved children, as she used to say.

But she couldn't help it, she told me. And she didn't want to try, either. Fornicating for fun, as she said, was a privilege that men had enjoyed for centuries. Women could do it too these days without being whores. Everyone falls in love now and then, she said. And even more banal: It's possible to love several people at the same time on different levels. You don't love your parents in the same way as your children. Or your lover the same way as your husband. And the wonderful remark: Just because you make love to someone doesn't mean you love him. Of course she also said: You're free too. As a responsible person you can sleep with other people too if you need to or get the urge.

During the first few years I did, once in a while. It wasn't very satisfying for either person involved. I couldn't think of anything except that I was just doing it because, in a way, I was supposed to do it. The world almost expected it of me. And yet the simple truth was that Charlotte was the only person I wanted to go to bed with.

Charlotte couldn't hide her affairs. She didn't want to either, she said, even though she did actually try to at the beginning of each new one. We had late-night discussions about the affairs and the nature of love. That was usually when she was starting to get tired of the guy. Then we made love, cried, and talked.

She wouldn't dream of leaving me. She loved me and I was the father of her children. Most of those so-called macho men were disappointing in bed, she said. Then what the hell did she want with them? I don't know.

It killed me every time she got that special glint in her eye, a look of almost lascivious desperation. Tenderness would radiate from her skin. She would get happy and excited. She got so damned beautiful. Her skin seemed to glow. Signs that had made me ache for her when we were first together, because they were reserved for me and (I have to admit) my member. I know what male pride is all about. Every time she had an affair, a "love interlude" as she called it, I found myself thinking: Is he better than me? And no matter how many times she told me I was a wonderful lover, I still felt a nagging doubt.

I couldn't take it when she and her girlfriends talked about men as studs. I didn't think of women as objects anymore, but women were thinking of us that way. I couldn't stand that closed world that women had created in the 70s, a world we were excluded from. They took away our privileges and then in the same breath adopted them themselves. We were left standing there with our pants down around our ankles, whimpering and afraid. Henrik and I had long talks about that.

In the meantime, other men were going on as if nothing had happened. They were just as self-centered and egotistical as men have always been. Sex role problems weren't keeping them awake at night. For them, equality meant helping with the dishes. And a lot of our liberated women fell for them, time after time. Not because they wanted to live with them. Then what for? To have their souls abused? And then to return to their gentle husband at home who would be understanding? Was it because freedom would only be fully realized if they used it in a physical way? I don't know.

We stayed together.

Once in a while I hated Charlotte so intensely that I could

have hit her. But I never did. She always came back; she never left me completely. We were crazy about our two kids, even though they had both come along almost accidentally during a break from the Pill. I was constantly crazy about them, Charlotte only off and on. She mainly thought about herself and her dazzling career as a journalist. But at times that gave her a guilty conscience too. Then she would try to spend so much time with the children that they got totally confused by all the pampering, attention, and concern their mother heaped on them. After a couple of days life would go back to normal and the star reporter would return heart and soul to the TV news department.

Sitting in the plane on my way to claim my wife's body in Spain, my primary feeling was not sorrow but relief.

I'm not ashamed that I was relieved and that for the first time in many years I felt free and unafraid. The fear of being hurt was suddenly gone. I could never be sure of what she might do or where I stood—whether she would leave me or not. When she was advancing as a journalist (which meant, among other things, that we moved around a lot), I broke off my studies in order to follow her. In the name of equality I took care of the children and encouraged my talented, beautiful wife.

So there I was—34 years old with a law degree that up to now had only provided me with a part-time job in the Ministry of Social Affairs, where I sat reconciling Common Market regulations. It was practical for one of us to have a part-time job. So I was the one, and I have to admit that I often enjoyed it. By the time Charlotte finally reached her highest goal, the evening news, I had been totally and completely reduced to being the husband of the well-known TV journalist, Charlotte Damsborg.

It didn't bother me that I was going to be alone with the children. I had been alone with them often, whenever Charlotte took off on one of her numerous assignments. I was going to miss her terribly, but I missed her when she was alive too.

My situation isn't exceptional these days, even for a man.

And lots of women know all too well what my situation feels like. It's just that it wasn't always easy being one of the privileged few who got to feel the physical impact of this brave new world.

I felt light-headed and ordered a whiskey after the coffee and cognac. It was at that moment (not before, as many people have claimed) that I met Claes. I was convinced, at least at that time, that the meeting was accidental. He sat down in the seat next to me and lit a cigarette. The words that he uttered were not at all conspiratorial, as was also claimed later on.

The following is what he actually said, translated from Swedish:

"Hey friend, do you mind if I sit here and smoke? I'm in the non-smoking section and it's hell to have to sit there for four hours and not be able to smoke any cancer sticks. Thanks, buddy. You're Danish, aren't you?"

3

I liked Claes Hylander immediately. Charming in a straight-forward way. Built like Ingmar Stenmark. Journalist for the biggest Scandinavian newspaper, *Expressen*, where he worked as a foreign correspondent. Blond like an advertisement for Sweden, but with brawny arms in a short-sleeved American shirt. Charlotte would have called him sexy, I think. No, I know she would have. She probably would have fallen for him. Maybe it would be easier to get an impression of him by comparing him to me. I am of average height (5'9") with dark hair receding at the temples. Claes was almost 6'3" with straight blond hair. I have a full beard. He was clean-shaven with what novelists in the olden days used to call a firm jaw. I tend not to say much. He talked like a waterfall and was a good storyteller. Talked for the first fifteen minutes about himself, his job, and his travels. It sounded like he'd been almost everywhere.

He was one of those people you always picture making an entrance with a smile and a loud voice. There are lots of people like that in our crowd. He made me think of a scene in *The Godfather* where one of the mafiosi walks into a hotel suite in Las Vegas, dishing out compliments and friendly greetings to everyone. Even his worst enemy receives a smile and a warm handshake. His enemy repays him later by getting a hit man to shoot the clown right between the eyes. The symbol of American warmth and hospitality.

During a pause I managed to say, "I've read your columns in the Danish paper *Ekstra Bladet*, and I enjoyed them."

He thanked me for the compliment and ordered more whiskey for us. What was I going to Spain for? I told him straight
out. I'd been drinking. Normally I keep my mouth shut around
strangers.

He had known her, he said. In what way, I asked myself, but
said nothing except a polite "Oh, really?"

"She was a nice girl. And a damn good journalist. It's a hell
of a world we live in. And you have children, don't you?"

"Yes, we have two." Did he know her that well?

"It's really shitty the amount of crap you hear about these
days. She was a hell of a journalist. I've worked with her many
times. Most women are so damn sentimental in their work, but
not Charlotte. She was tough and got straight to the point."

He was starting to irritate me, but before I could say anything, the stewardess arrived with the drinks. We drank a toast
and he shook his head and said "damn" a few more times.
I didn't feel like hearing about Charlotte's journalistic or other
possible exploits abroad, so I asked in a neutral tone what
he thought about the Basque situation and their demands for
autonomy.

"Nothing," he said. "I write about them, but I think they're
raving maniacs. That's why I'm such a damn good journalist.
Everyone admires my objectivity."

That surprised me. Most Danish journalists are far from
apolitical. I've witnessed numerous heated discussions among
Charlotte and her colleagues about the necessity of becoming
involved. I mentioned that to Claes Hylander.

"The Danes are a little soft. Kind of sentimental. Blood is
ketchup to them, revolutions are totally foreign. Rage is a rarity
and softness is a virtue. Kindness is too strong a part of your
character for you to really understand what evil is."

Suddenly I realized that he'd had quite a lot to drink. His
eyes looked blank for a moment — then he said, "Who the hell
would want to blow up a beautiful girl like Charlotte?"

"I thought you only knew her as a colleague."

He was silent. Scowled like my almost-five-year-old son when he gets caught doing something he knows is wrong.

"What do you mean?" he asked with a smile that made his eyes look different again. They were bloodshot but very blue. Charlotte would probably have said that he would look great on TV, which in her prosaic world was the closest anyone could come to godliness.

"I don't know. I guess I'm a little out of it."

"But she's dead now, isn't she?" he said with unnecessary cruelty — journalists aren't always the most subtle or tactful kind of people. He went on, "But you know how it is sometimes when you're off away from home. You know how it is, don't you?"

"No, I don't. I usually stay home."

"Oh yeah, that's right."

In the new pause we both drank our whiskey.

"You were going to say something," I said then.

"Yeah. I don't know . . . but she's dead now, isn't she?"

I didn't say anything.

"And it was a couple of years ago, after all."

"That you happened to be working together, and because you happened to be feeling lonely, you just happened to go to bed with each other?" I tried to sound sarcastic.

"Now listen here, friend. That's not what I meant."

"What did you mean, then? You mean it isn't true?"

"It wasn't anything special."

"Do you mean to imply that my wife wasn't anything special in bed?"

I now found myself in what Charlotte often had described as my self-torture corner. Once when she had been drinking, she said that I had not only adopted many positive female characteristics, but I had also assumed a lot of the masochistic traits of women in the past. And that I enjoyed being that way. That was one of the remarks I promised myself I would never forgive her for, and now for the first time, in the roar of the airplane, I thought about the humiliation. And at the same moment I remembered another accusation she'd tossed at me during that fight: "You pick up identities the way the Salvation Army picks up other people's old clothes."

"Well, what did you mean? Isn't it true, what I said?" I kept at him.

"But my dear friend. She has just died, you know. What are you getting at?"

"Just answer me. It means a lot to me . . . but it doesn't mean a damn thing either."

He suddenly looked completely sober.

"What the hell. We only slept together once. It doesn't mean anything. That's what happens when people are lonely. When they're bored. These days people do it just for fun. You know that."

"Quit telling me what I'm supposed to know," I replied to his comforting words for the cuckold. In the past it was forbidden to sin. Now it's forbidden to be bored. Suddenly I felt very tired.

"Can't you find somewhere else to smoke?"

"Sure." He squeezed his way out. "Yeah . . . it's really a bunch of crap."

"Thanks for the drink," I said, looking over the grubby headrest to watch him go down the aisle toward the non-smoking section. He said something to the stewardess, who put her head back and smiled without moving her face away when his hand gently, but quick as a magician, stroked her cheek.

I didn't have time to get seriously annoyed. The usual ritual surrounding a plane-landing began, and shortly afterwards I saw him climb into the bus waiting near the plane. I stopped, then went slowly down the stairs, and got a seat all the way back near the door. He stood holding on to a strap over by the driver, talking animatedly with some woman. She leaned back and laughed up into his face.

I've often heard people say that they're seized by a special feeling of lightness whenever they land in a new place. Something to do with the infinite possibilities opening before them. As if they acquire a new personality because they move their physical body a few thousand kilometers. I get tired, cranky, and homesick. The whiskey had begun to burn in my stomach; I felt lost and depressed. The bus pitched and shook and belched black diesel smoke, and I started to feel carsick on the short ride. Claes towered over the other passengers, who, even though they looked tired, were talking loudly about Madrid, which lay somewhere out in the fog. It was overcast, windy, and cold.

We drove up to the arrival hall. The *guardia civil* were still wearing their weird black hats and green uniforms and carrying submachine guns, even though the dictator was dead, and there were just as many cigarette butts scattered over the floor of the passport control as before. I felt more and more depressed, and I missed my kids.

We whisked through the passport control and into the baggage area. So something *had* changed since Franco's death, although the men with the leather souls appeared to be the same as before.

The loudspeaker crackled in Spanish. I didn't catch the message. Then it came in English. A union dispute was going on. The personnel were working according to regulations and we shouldn't expect our baggage to be delivered for a couple of hours. The crowd uttered a collective moan. I saw Claes coming toward me and I moved away demonstratively. I could see that he smiled, but I didn't care. The loudspeaker crackled again. This time I caught the message in Spanish. It was the same one as before, but now Iberia apologized for the delay.

A youngish man in a gray suit that bagged at the knees was
making his way through the passengers who hadn't been lucky
enough to find a place to sit. He came toward me. I tried to look
hostile. The alcohol was disappearing from my system all too
quickly. My stomach felt like it was full of acid. He headed
straight for me.

"Mr. Jensen? Mr. Poul Jensen?" he asked in Danish. His
voice was pleasant, cultured, with a touch of dialect — a hint of
Jysk.

I nodded.

"Lars Hansen, the Danish embassy." A dry, quick handshake. "Welcome to Spain. I'm sorry that the occasion is so
regrettable. I'm very sorry about your wife."

Again I simply nodded.

"I've explained your situation to Iberia, and both they and
the authorities have been very cooperative. This strike is the
negative side of democracy; the more, shall we say, 'friendly'
attitude of the police is the positive side." He smiled. "Your
baggage won't be put on the carousel, so if you'll come with me,
we'll go straight through customs and you can identify your
suitcase."

"That's very kind of you." And I meant it. I was properly
impressed. He acted like he knew what he was doing even
though he wasn't any older than me. I said, "I understood that
my contact man at the Danish embassy was supposed to be a
Mr. Simonsen."

He took me lightly by the arm. "That's right, but unfortunately he's ill. It's this way to customs."

As we left, Claes raised his hand and smiled. I couldn't resist
looking back at him and had to smile too when I saw a little glass
appear in his big hand. He'd apparently started in on the duty-
free goods, to pass the time while he waited.

We walked right through customs. The inspector seemed

totally uninterested. Lars Hansen showed him a paper with the seal of the Danish Crown. Franco really was dead. My suitcase was right outside. I couldn't understand how it had gotten there so fast. Lars Hansen grabbed hold of it and walked effortlessly toward the automatic doors as I followed through the crush of humanity waiting for the other passengers.

Outside the wind was cold, just like in Denmark. The clouds were breaking up on the horizon, but spring was still a long way off. I followed the embassy man over to a yellow Seat-127. The license plates were Spanish. It had a black antenna sticking up. Lars Hansen threw my suitcase into the trunk and got in behind the wheel before opening the door for me. He put on his seat belt.

"It's an old habit," he said. "From Denmark, you know. Down here it's only required outside the cities, but the way they drive..." He let the sentence hang and maneuvered confidently through the traffic, which was light. Siesta, I presumed. The usual red-and-black, junky rattletrap Seat taxis. I smiled a little at myself over the word "usual." As if I were a world traveler.

Lars Hansen interrupted my train of thought by asking, "You know Madrid, perhaps?" I was glad that he had enough tact not to mention Charlotte and twist the knife in the wound.

"I haven't been here for several years. But in the early 70s I was here a lot. With Charlotte. But then we had a baby."

He didn't say anything. The city really hadn't changed all that much. The apartment blocks had spread farther out. They were brown and ugly. There were more political posters, more cars, more dirt than I remembered, and the smog lay over the city like a scowl. I told him about my impressions.

"Well no," he said. "It's more crowded, more full of cars. Crazier but still just as wonderful."

"Have you been here a long time?"

"Almost three years. I'll probably be transferred before long."

"Where to?"

"A stint at home and then out to a new post somewhere. Part of the charm of the job, if you will." He had edged over into the left lane and was driving fast but confidently. Used the rearview mirror adeptly and seemed both preoccupied and extremely intense at the same time. I felt more at ease. My stomach had settled down. I almost began to feel that it was nice being on a trip, even though Charlotte with the Swede kept popping up in my mind in quick, painful flashes. In silence we let ourselves be swallowed up by the city; we drove past the monumental greenish-foaming fountain in Plaza Colón before he spoke again.

"We've booked you at the Hotel Sideral. Does that sound familiar?"

"No."

"It's centrally located, right behind the Prado by Retiro Park — places that you probably remember. Neat and clean and not too expensive. It's fine for just one night. Then we'll get you on your way tomorrow."

I thanked him. And that was it. We didn't say anything else to each other until we got out in front of the hotel, which was on a side street. He took my suitcase and went into the lobby. The clerk at the front desk seemed to be expecting him, seemed to know him. Everything was done in brown. You could see into the bar and there was a lit-up neon sign that said "Bingo" over the stairway to the second floor.

"The latest fad down here — the modern world," he explained, as I handed in my passport and signed on the dotted line on the hotel's yellow check-in form.

"Room 367." The clerk smiled and said welcome and pressed a button so that a fifteen-year-old boy would take my suitcase.

Lars Hansen went up with me. "To see that you're com-
fortably settled. That's my responsibility, you know."

The room was large and neat — a small living room and a
separate bedroom with a black-and-white TV. The colors were a
ghastly brown and red, but it looked clean. Lars Hansen gave
the boy a tip. I sat down on a chair. He stood with the car keys in
his hand, tossing them up and down.

"Mr. Jensen. Would you like to have dinner with me this
evening somewhere in town? I'm a bachelor and it's nice to talk
with a countryman fresh from home. Of course . . . if you'd
rather be alone, go to bed early . . . ?"

I was suddenly very grateful, both for his offer and for his
tact and silence. So I said I'd like to very much.

"Then I'll pick you up at 8 o'clock. You probably remember
that people eat late here, but we can have a drink first."

And then he left. Like a shadow he was gone and I couldn't
remember what he looked like. A nice face, a gray suit. Was his
hair dark or just plain brown? It's details that I notice most. His
cuticles were torn, as if someone had scratched at his skin.

I got out the whiskey that I'd bought at the airport and lay
down on the bed with the bottle. The last thing I thought about
before I fell asleep was my kids.

4

I woke up feeling scared. Not of anything in particular, just scared. At first I didn't dare get up. I sat there shaking with my legs tucked up to my chin. Then I went out to the bathroom and took a shower. Let the water pound hard all over my body. I was cold and didn't really wake up until I was toweling myself off in front of the mirror and the unmade bed. I saw a pinched white face under a mane of dark, tousled hair — hazily because my glasses were lying on the nightstand with my watch. My mouth was dry but I didn't dare drink the water.

It was 7:30. I rang the switchboard and explained in my slow, laborious, ungrammatical Spanish that I wanted to put through a phone call to Denmark. I gave her Helle and Henrik's number. Read off the numbers one by one, first in Spanish and then in English. Doing something practical helped; it took me away to Gentofte. Were the children all right? Had they taken their bath yet? Were they going to bed soon? Had they eaten dinner? Did someone read them a good-night story? How were they surviving without me? The longest I'd ever been away from them was two days. And the youngest one was only four months old then.

The switchboard operator changed over to English. She would call me back as soon as she got a connection. All the lines were busy. I smoked a cigarette and got dressed. Then I smoked another one and the telephone rang. It was the man from the embassy. I had forgotten his name.

"Lars Hansen. Good evening. Did you get some sleep?"

"Yes, I did," I said.

There was silence at the other end.

"Yes, thanks. I slept well." My heart was pounding hard.

"That's good. I'm down in the lobby. I'll wait for you in the bar."

"As a matter of fact I've just put in a call to Denmark."

"That's no problem. I'll tell the switchboard that you're in the bar. So long."

He hung up.

I couldn't figure out how to pull up the blinds, but I took a coat along because I remembered how cold it had been in the afternoon. I waited a while, hoping that the phone would ring. Then I left the room and walked down the three flights. The carpet was old; the pattern had yellow woven in with the red. The walls were a dirty yellow.

The switchboard operator looked up from her magazine and nodded to me. The bar was right off the lobby. The man from the embassy was standing at the bar, half-sitting on the high brown barstool. The waiters were dressed in green jackets. People in nice clothes were sitting at round tables with faded yellow tablecloths and talking loudly with each other. The usual scene was being played out along the steel edge of the bar. Glasses clinked. Dishes were slammed down hard. The floor in front of the bar was covered with napkins, cigarette butts, and scraps of food. On my way over to him, I polished my glasses on my handkerchief. He hadn't changed his clothes. The same gray suit with the baggy knees. I slid onto the stool next to him.

"What would you like?" he asked. "Sherry, or something stronger?"

He caught the waiter's eye but I ordered a beer myself, savoring the little dry plop when the waiter, with a deft gesture, put down the beer coaster with its printed advertisement for SKOL. I took a long swallow and immediately felt better. Not until then did we toast each other, and Lars Hansen said, "If you don't mind, I think we'll eat at a little working-class restaurant I know. Though 'little' is perhaps not quite the right word for it. It's Galician." He took another sip of his drink. "Do you like shellfish? Good. Watch out for the dessert though — it can be rather intoxicating. But let's enjoy ourselves this evening. You look a little tired. Maybe we should just get the practical matters out of the way."

He drank some more. It looked like gin and tonic. He leaned closer. I had the feeling that we were standing there arranging something dirty or underhanded. He spoke in a low voice, as if he didn't want the people in the bar to hear what he was saying. It seemed unnecessary. His fingers with the ragged cuticles were holding a filter cigarette. He hadn't shaved, either. There was a faint shadow on his chin.

"We've bought you a plane ticket to San Sebastián. The flight leaves around noon. I have the ticket with me. We could put it in your box at the desk, couldn't we? Unfortunately we only have an honorary consul in San Sebastián, but I've taken the liberty of contacting one of my personal friends. He will be happy to help you with the practical business."

I thanked him and said that he was being too kind.

"Don't mention it. He's an attorney. He'll take care of the details so you can claim your wife's body. And we'll take care of what's required on this end. Once again: I am very sorry."

Again I didn't know what to say to this incomprehensible fact, so instead I said, "Actually, I'm hungry. It's way past Danish dinner time, and children like to eat at 6 o'clock, you know."

He stared at me, astonished.

"Oh, I just mean — I have two kids, so I'm used to eating at 6 o'clock."

He laughed. "Well, I guess there isn't anything else to discuss. I'll go ask about your phone call to Denmark. Shall we finish our drinks?"

He left. I stayed and drank my beer. I wasn't especially hungry. The smoke from the black tobacco irritated my nose. The waiters worked quickly and efficiently, shouting the orders to their colleagues behind the bar. I tried to concentrate on relearning the words they were using, to recall the Spanish words that must be somewhere in the back of my mind. The man from the embassy returned.

"I'm sorry, Mr. Jensen. There's at least a two-hour wait to Denmark. Basque terrorists blew up a telephone building a few days ago. It's been really impossible lately."

"They're really going at it, aren't they?" I said. "Wives and telephone buildings. What is it they want, these people?"

"Don't ask me. It's a rather complicated situation. Do you want to wait for the phone call?"

"No. Could you tell the operator that I'll try again later this evening?"

"Certainly."

We took care of the necessary details on our way out. While I was signing a receipt to have my Eurochecks and the pink Iberia ticket placed in a safe deposit box, I heard him in the background speaking to the switchboard operator in a rapid, precise Spanish. Then we went out into the wet evening.

We turned left down a sloping street. A single taxi was waiting in front of the parked cars. A green light indicated that it was free, but we didn't take it. The man from the embassy walked past it without a word. The buildings were shuttered and looked hostile. He took a skip in order to fall into step with me. The asphalt gleamed black with rain. There was a fence ahead of us. Behind it I suddenly recognized the Prado. The fence was brilliantly lit. A cloak-clad officer walked with a submachine gun held upright in front of him. It was a dark evening. You could hear the roar of the traffic not so far away, but except for the officer in the dark cloak, there wasn't a soul in sight.

We walked quickly, down past the Prado's dark façade. Two

of the *guardia civil* were stomping their feet in front of the closed gate, but down on the *paseo* there were more people and heavier traffic. A forest of umbrellas was moving along in the dark evening. We talked about neutral subjects. About Madrid. About traveling and about my kids. I had the feeling that he was drawing me out, that he was sincerely trying to get to know me. He pointed out the Parliament, where a number of the *guardia civil* had attempted a coup. He showed me the new Senate across from the luxury Palace Hotel.

There were long pauses in our conversation. In a bar we stood lost in our own thoughts, staring into the mirror behind the bartender while we drank small glasses of red wine. We walked through the narrow streets. All of the bars were full. People stood jammed against the counters eating *tapas*. I remembered them well. When Charlotte and I were quite young, in our first magical time together, we lived in Madrid for two weeks on love and cheap *tapas*: octopus, meat on a skewer, lettuce, potatoes, and bread.

The man from the embassy ordered a clay bowl full of shrimp in garlic and another couple of glasses of wine. My legs were tired, but we stood at the bar in a packed crowd. The black tobacco stung my eyes. I was on my twentieth cigarette of the day. With a light hold on my elbow he led me down toward Puerta del Sol, which looked familiar.

We crossed the plaza and stood facing a massive building of red and yellow brick. At the very top there was a tiny bell. The clock face underneath showed almost 9 o'clock. Officers with machine guns stood at each corner of the building. They shivered in the cold under their brown capes. People rushed by, ignoring their presence. Although it had stopped raining, I noticed that the magazines and newspapers were still covered with plastic in front of the kiosk on the plaza. The wind tore at the plastic, which was fastened with clips. The traffic was heavy and slow. Everything gray on gray, streaked like ashes.

The man from the embassy said, "This is Puerta del Sol."
He pointed toward the massive building with the bell tower.
"And that's the headquarters of the Security Police. From here
orders go out all over Spain. All roads in the kingdom lead here,
to the zero-kilometer stone. This is where the country is ruled
from, with the same firm hand that has always ruled it since the
Catholic kings united this part of the Iberian peninsula."

I stamped my feet to get warm.

"Screams of terror used to come from there, under Franco,"
I said. Behind me I heard a plaintive shouting. I turned around.
There was a man standing under a blue umbrella, his chest
covered with multicolored lottery tickets. Instead of eyes, he had
two bulging flaps of flesh, streaked with blue lines. Mournfully
he droned out his numbers, while the man from the embassy
talked on, ignoring him.

"Many things are unchanged in this country." He rattled off
something in Spanish that I didn't understand. "The same dogs
with different collars, as they say in Spanish. It's the same
people who decide. The same ones who wield the whip."

"Do you really mean that? You've just shown me the Parliament. A socialist government is in power . . ."

He stared at me almost angrily. A second lottery-ticket
vendor set up next to the man with no eyes. She was quite
young, and she was wall-eyed. The man and the girl took turns
singing their mournful tune.

"Social-democratic. That's something different. There's
only democracy for the rulers here. It's a superficial kind of
democracy. You yourself said that screams of terror used to
come from that building. You might just as well have said that
screams of terror are *still* coming from it. A lot of false confes-
sions are still beaten out of people in the cellars of Puerta del
Sol."

A woman with a sleeping child lay wrapped in blankets on
the wet pavement. The woman had her left hand stretched out,

begging silently. The child's naked, misshapen foot stuck out of
the dirty rags. A few coins lay glinting with moisture in front of
the child's grotesque foot.

"Is that the kind of ideas the Danish embassy presents to
visitors these days?" I asked. Political discussions bore me, but
Charlotte had often told me that diplomats are reactionary —
often more reactionary than the government itself — so his
views surprised me. He didn't seem to hear me.

"Look around you, Mr. Jensen. What do you see?" He let
his hand sweep over the throngs of people, as if he wanted to
gather up the beggars, the lottery-ticket vendors, the street
hawkers with their cheap, screeching cassette tapes with gaily
colored boxes and scratched contents, the smell of hamburgers,
sausages, and cheap oil, and all the well-dressed people on their
way out to dinner. His jacket sleeve stuck out of his coat. A
thread was unraveling at the edge. "Look around you! This is
the world's ninth or tenth largest industrial power, and there are
people in Andalusia who go to bed hungry every night. There
are people in Euskadi who are tortured for protesting against
nuclear power. And social problems are solved in two ways: with
tear gas and smoke bombs or by issuing the poor a bunch of
lottery tickets. Is that democracy?"

Small drops of rain struck my shoulder.

"I don't know. The first way certainly isn't. But I can't believe that people are made totally powerless when at least they're
allowed to sell lottery tickets. That's a means of existence too. A
way of participating, of earning their own living. What do we do
at home? We buy our way right out of all our social differences.
Which is better in the long run? Don't ask me."

Now he was looking directly at me. There was anger in his
eyes. The rain hit me on the back of the neck again. The
umbrellas blossomed like flowers.

"You have some strange ideas in Denmark sometimes. Why is it you always make the poverty in the south seem picturesque? Something you can write about on a postcard. Poor, but happy, isn't that right?"

"What do you mean, 'you'?"

It started raining harder. The lottery-ticket sellers retreated into a doorway, but their shouts were just as loud. The sleeping child stirred but continued to lie there, and people moved around the woman and child without noticing them. People were still pouring out of the entrance to the Metro station. They all looked like they were surprised it was raining.

" 'You'?" I repeated to his rigid face. I imagined that he was clenching his fists in his coat pockets. "What do you mean, 'you'? That's no way to argue — denying your Danishness just because you live abroad."

He smiled, seemed to relax.

"Excuse me. I got too excited. I shouldn't bother you with my private opinions." The rain struck his face, but he just now seemed to realize it had started to rain again. He became paternal again, dropping the subject.

"But you're getting wet — let's take a cab and get some food and wine. There's something healthy about trying out your opinions on a fellow countryman once in a while. It's as if you see them in a different perspective, don't you think?"

Actually, I hadn't really contradicted him all that much, but I let it go with a shrug and a smile. I try to avoid confrontations.

We went over to the line of waiting cabs. On our way up narrow streets, in slow, heavy traffic, we each sat in our own corner, without speaking. I didn't know where we were driving to, but we were let off on the corner of a dimly-lit street. We walked less than twenty yards and stepped into a noisy, hot room with glaring lights. There was a small bar. People were standing

packed together, with wine glasses in their hands. In the back
there was a little passageway that apparently led into the restaurant itself. Claes was standing at the middle of the bar with a
glass of wine in his hand. He caught sight of us right away.

"I'll be damned. It's a small world. If it isn't Poul. Come and
have a drink, and later we'll eat shellfish till we burst," he said
in his pan-Scandinavian. "Come and meet a couple of my
British colleagues. They knew your wife well. Goddamn those
barbarians who blew her up... Who's your silent friend?
Shane? Or Franco's ghost? Red or white? Take the red. It
doubles your blood cells in ten minutes. The white tastes like
piss. Damn this country! ¡Qué país! It's so cold! And they call
this the south!"

The sentences came in rapid spurts. In many ways I guess I
seemed more Swedish than he did.

It was the man from the embassy who replied. "I think Mr.
Jensen would like to take it a little easy tonight," he said, stepping between us.

"Like hell he does. He can't go around moping on his first
night in Madrid. That won't bring back the dead. If you eat
shellfish in a bad mood, it'll turn to poison in your blood. But
eating shellfish in a good mood is a pick-me-up that you Danish
social democrats should introduce in the nurseries, the schools,
and the government. Watch out you don't wind up with a society like the Swedes have. I bet pretty soon we'll have to shit on
command in Sweden!"

He stepped around the man from the embassy and took my
arm. He ordered wine and introduced me to his two British
colleagues, who mumbled something sympathetic before going
back to their discussion about some Spanish politician.

The man from the embassy had turned white in the face.

"Let's just have dinner together," I said to cool things off.

"Who's your friend, Poul?" asked Claes.

"Lars Hansen, the Danish embassy. Claes . . . ?"

"Hylander. Claes Hylander, *Expressen*. I don't think we've met. I've never even heard your name before."

"We don't have that much to do with Swedish journalists either."

"How true. How true. Red or white?"

Lars Hansen pulled himself together. Soon he was involved in the discussion about the Spanish politician's future or lack thereof. I kept getting a refilled glass of wine in my hand somehow. I emptied them one after the other. Once in a while Claes handed me a piece of smoked ham. I stood there as if under a bell jar.

Behind the bar a hard-working kitchen helper arranged one big platter of shellfish after another. His forehead was covered with sweat, which ran down through the hairs on his arms. Crab, lobster, shrimp, claws and strange growths piled up on the platters before they were carried off. In the corner sat an old woman with a white apron, toothless gums, and lottery tickets like rows of medals on her breast. I began to feel better and better. Finally a waiter with sweat pouring down his face came to say that our table was ready now. The heat was tremendous.

They kept bringing us wine as we chomped on shellfish and bread. Claes Hylander talked non-stop. Lars Hansen got quieter and quieter. He kept calling me Mr. Jensen even though I started calling him Lars. In spite of his youth, there was an old-fashioned air about him. I can't really remember what we discussed, but I recall that at one point I talked about my kids at great length to a polite, blank British face.

The restaurant was packed to the walls. The dessert turned out to be a grayish liquid in a deep dish, which had a fine layer of sugar on the bottom. The waiter struck a match and blue flames flared up. Claes Hylander lifted the spoon and carried the flames with it like a magician at the marketplace. His eyes were red, and I remember clearly that at one point, in the middle of a sentence in English, he turned toward the man from the embassy.

"How many years did you say you'd been at the Danish embassy, my friend?"

"I didn't say." He smiled.

Claes let the flames lick along the spoon. "Well?"

"Well what?"

"How many years have you been at the Danish embassy?"

"Almost three."

Claes kept on stirring the dessert. He stared at the man from the embassy, who took a sip of mineral water from his glass.

"It's funny that I've never met you. I have called on our sister embassy, you know."

"You couldn't have met everyone who works at the embassy. You must have to work now and then too, Mr. Hylander."

Claes kept on stirring. His red eyes stared at the man from the embassy. The British journalists had stopped talking.

" 'Mr.'! You and your 'Mr.'! Scandinavians don't say 'Mr.' to each other anymore. What kind of a weirdo are you, 'Mr. Hansen'?"

"It's not very pleasant listening to you."

Claes balanced the spoon between two fingers and then let it fall into the burning liquid. Small drops of fire sprayed out over the table. The man from the embassy jerked his arm away, and Claes burst out laughing.

"You know what this is, Mister? It's good 120-proof Galician alcohol, sugar, and fire. And now just watch what happens." He clapped his hands and the waiter came with an old-fashioned tin coffee pot and poured black coffee into the flaming alcohol. The fire died out slowly. The man from the embassy stared straight ahead. I was sitting with my wine glass in my hand when the waiter divided up the dessert in coffee cups.

"*Queimada!*" said Claes. "*Queimada.* It means 'burned.'
Burned like in hell." Again he stared straight at the man from
the embassy. Then he turned toward me, lifted his cup, and said
"skål." It tasted sweet and good. My face felt even hotter.

"Well, Mr. Poul Jensen. So are you going to pick up Charlotte's body in San Sebastián?" The question came so brutally
that I started to laugh.

"Sure, Mr. Ex-Lover. The cuckold is going to pick up his
wife's body in San Sebastián tomorrow."

Lars Hansen tried to say something, but Claes turned to him
and told him to shut up.

"I think we should go now," said the man from the embassy.

"I said shut up!" Claes raised his cup and took another gulp.
My eyes started to water.

"How about if you and I — husband and lover — go to San
Sebastián together in my car tomorrow?"

"Mr. Jensen can't do that," said the man from the embassy.

"Mr. Jensen can't do that, huh . . . Has Mr. Jensen lost his
voice? Maybe Mr. Jensen has lost his wife and his voice and his
own free will."

Lars Hansen got up.

"Now you're going too far, Mr. Hylander. You're drunk and
unpleasant."

But Claes completely ignored him and turned to me instead.
I was still laughing like an idiot.

"What do you say?"

"That might be fun. We could sit in the car and tell bedtime
stories about Charlotte."

"Look here, Mr. Jensen. You already have a ticket to San
Sebastián tomorrow. We've made various arrangements for you.
This makes things very difficult."

"Have you paid for the ticket?" Claes asked me.

"The embassy paid for it."

"OK, then the embassy can get it refunded. So there's nothing more to discuss."

"I must protest. I think you should stick to the original plans."

"Now you shut up!" yelled Claes. The two British journalists and several of the people at neighboring tables had started to shift uneasily in their seats; they were staring at us. I drank some more dessert and everything began to swim a little. I felt very tired.

"I'd better take the plane."

Claes turned away. "Do what you want. Maybe I'll see you up there."

The man from the embassy sat down again. I could hardly stay in my chair. Claes ignored both of us completely and talked only to the two journalists from England or the U.K. or whatever country they were from. Shortly afterwards, we evidently got the bill. I remember dark streets and rain and the smell of black tobacco in a taxi, and I remember that the man from the embassy held me up, got the key, and sent me up in the elevator.

I lay down on the bed. The walls of the room began to revolve. There was a man standing behind the curtain, pointing a gun at me. I got out of bed and tore open the curtain, but he'd apparently vanished in the meantime. He wasn't in the bathroom. I looked in the closet too. Then I picked up the phone. Now I wanted to talk to my kids.

Oddly enough it was the same switchboard operator. In laborious English I asked for a connection to Denmark. The walls of the room kept on getting closer, but just as they were about to crush me, they retreated again. The woman asked me sharply whether I was serious this time. I asked her what she meant by that. Quite angry, she explained that last time I had asked my friend to cancel the phone call just as she had gotten through to the Danish operator. I asked her what friend she was talking about.

"Your Spanish friend from this evening. The one who brought you home, *señor!*"

"He's just as Danish as I am. He's from the Danish embassy."

"I know a Spaniard when I see one, *señor.* You can make your call tomorrow. *Buenas noches.*"

The line went dead. I sat for a long time with the telephone in my hand, while the walls continued their rhythmic dance and the man with the gun behind the curtain kept an eye on every move I made.

5

I woke up with a salty taste in my mouth, but my head was clear. It wasn't very late. I couldn't find my watch. All I noticed was a hollow feeling; something was missing. It was my kids. I'd been gone one whole day, and the truth was, I missed them. I hardly gave Charlotte a second thought. I picked up the phone, but just before the static on the line was replaced by the operator's voice, I changed my mind. Something was wrong.

I put down the receiver, splashed some water on my face, and put on some clothes. I walked down the three flights of stairs. It wasn't more than 8 o'clock, but the lobby was already full of people. A group of Japanese was in the middle of an elaborate bowing ceremony that looked like an elegant ballet. I slipped past them, but from the front desk I heard in English: "You are leaving today, sir?"

A statement, a question — a threat? The back of my head was throbbing. My mouth was dry and prickly. "Later," I said, continuing toward the door. The doorman stepped forward, but not to open the door. He blocked my way.

"Where are you going, sir?" asked the man at the front desk as I passed. He was standing very stiffly. I kept on going toward the doorman, who only at the last moment stepped aside and opened the double glass doors. First one of them and then, reluctantly, the other. "Are you coming back soon?"

I didn't answer but stepped out into the cold morning, took a deep breath, and began to run down the street. I felt the doorman's eyes on my back. I was soon out of breath and slowed down to a walk. One of the black-and-red Seat taxis rumbled past with the green letters LIBRE on a movable sign in the window. I flagged him down and got into the back seat. My lungs ached, and from both armpits trickled drops of sweat, rank as the butter from my childhood summers before we had a refrigerator. I asked to be driven to the telephone and telegraph office. With his right hand the driver dropped the flag and shifted into gear. Up by the main entrance to the hotel I saw the doorman pointing toward my cab, and a man started running over to a parked car, an Escort, which was parked under a no parking sign across from the hotel.

"Which telephone and telegraph office?" the taxi driver asked. A picture of the madonna dangled on a short metal chain from the rear view mirror. She was accompanied by a flabby woman and three fat children in a picture frame on the dashboard.

"The one at the closest post office, and hurry!"

He shrugged and drove off, gliding past the Prado and up toward Plaza Cibeles. I remembered the post office; it looks like a wedding cake. The morning traffic was heavy and we crept along in little spurts. I was sweating so my shirt stuck to my back even though it was a raw, gray morning.

He turned left in front of the post office. The fountain was dead. Paper blew across the plaza, and the radio spouted sports news at breakneck speed. We drove up a ways, and then he stopped. I looked back; the traffic was rolling by slowly, but it seemed to me that the yellow Escort hesitated, and then slid in toward the curb. The cars behind honked angrily.

"Why are we stopping?" I asked. The driver didn't answer, just pointed to a sign: *telefónica*. After I paid him I noticed that it didn't open until 9 o'clock. The yellow Escort still hadn't moved, in spite of the loud protests of the other cars. There were more and more cars belching and sputtering past.

My lungs, throat, and eyes were stinging. Now the yellow

Escort started moving toward me. Suddenly I saw there were
two people in the car, and it stopped right near where I was
standing. The window was slowly rolled down, but there was a
gap in the traffic, and amid blaring horns I ran straight across
the street. I kept going in the opposite direction from the Escort,
back toward Plaza Cibeles. I ran only fifty yards, then stopped
another cab and asked to be taken to the Palace Hotel. It was the
same driver who had just dropped me off. He must have turned
around right away. I threw 100 pesetas at him, jumped out of
the cab again, and started running down a side street. There
were practically no people around. Black plastic cans stood in
groups with garbage spilling out over the edges in obscene
colors. I ran another fifty yards, then I couldn't go on. An
elderly woman in black looked up from where she was sitting on
the sidewalk with a tray of cigarettes. Her shawl slipped from her
face, revealing toothless gums. She stretched out her hand, and
I had to stop myself from taking off again.

When I looked back there was no one in sight, and I ducked
into a bar. "Coffee!" I said, indicating with my hands that I
wanted to have coffee with milk in a big glass. "A double coffee.
And mineral water. A bottle!" They brought the bottle right
away, dripping with moisture, cool and refreshing from the
refrigerator. A little later they brought the coffee. The waiter
poured the warm milk over the espresso and apathetically
plopped two packets of sugar and a long teaspoon into the
saucer. The coffee was hot and good. It didn't matter that I was
standing there treading on cigarette butts, scraps of bread, and
sugar wrappers—the remains of breakfast from the early
morning rush.

I stopped shaking and drank my coffee while I kept an eye on
the door. I was the only customer in the whole café. One of
those new one-armed bandits with no arms called seductively

every so often with a little song. "Play me! Play me!" the machine hummed mechanically.

I ordered more water and at the same time found out that the Palace Hotel was located at the end of the street and then to the left. Very close.

I wasn't sweating so much anymore, and when I got out onto the street, there was no Escort. The old woman was still sitting there, so in order to show her that I was sane again, I went over to her and bought a pack of Chesterfields without filters, which miraculously enough she had. That was a good omen. She had no teeth. She had tiny blue eyes and her face was nothing but wrinkles. She sat on the curb, dressed completely in black with a green apron and the tray in her lap. I paid what she asked and walked toward the hotel. The sidewalk was very narrow, but there weren't any cars coming.

It didn't take me more than five minutes to find the Palace Hotel. Didn't the Swede say that he was staying at the Palace? At the front desk they found his room number and pointed to a telephone where I could call him.

"Hello." He sounded far away — surly, tired, hung over, and disgusted. "Hello! Who's this?" I put down the phone. Because what could I really say to him? Then I went back to the front desk and asked if it would be possible to call Denmark even though I wasn't staying at the hotel. I let them know that I was waiting for Claes.

"Of course."

I went down a stairway and was directed to a telephone booth by the switchboard operator, who got me an outside line. She spoke English, too, as they had at the front desk. "The code number for Denmark is 45. Dial 07, wait for a new tone and then dial 45 followed by the city code and the telephone number." I thanked her profusely. She looked at me a little surprised as I turned on my heel and went into the warm calm of the booth and methodically dialed Helle's number in her plush suburb near Copenhagen.

Helle herself answered the phone. She sounded like she was just on her way out the door.

"Poul, is that you? We've been so worried about you. Where are you?"

"In Madrid, of course." Through the glass door I could look out at the switchboard operator sitting in front of her myriad of buttons, the headset over her ears, and the little microphone in front of her red mouth.

"What do you mean, of course?"

"How are the kids?"

"Fine. Great. Why didn't you contact the embassy?"

"What are you talking about? Someone from the embassy came and met me at the airport. What do the kids say about me being gone?"

Helle's voice came through loud and clear.

"That can't be right, Poul. I talked to the Danish embassy several times yesterday. They couldn't understand why you weren't at the airport, and they couldn't understand either why you didn't call and give them the name of your hotel."

"Now I get it," I said. Even though I really didn't. I hurried to say, "Everything's OK now, Helle. I have a chance to get a lift to San Sebastián today, so I can save the cost of a ticket."

"Who are you going to ride with?"

". . . and I'll call you when I get to San Sebastián."

"I asked you who you're going to ride with."

"And I asked you first: How are the kids?"

"I told you. They're fine. They asked for you this morning, but don't go around worrying about that. Who are you going to drive north with?"

"A Swedish journalist, Claes something-or-other from *Expressen*, and his photographer."

"Claes Hylander. Oh yeah, I know him well. He's all right." Now she sounded totally professional, like Charlotte, who was also on a first-name basis with lots of the foreign correspondents and reporters, whose names apparently often mean more than what they write. But I didn't say that to Helle. I also didn't say anything about the man from the embassy.

"Look, Helle, couldn't you call the foreign ministry and tell them that everything is OK and that I'll contact the Danish embassy from San Sebastián? They're not open yet, and I think we're going to leave pretty soon, and I don't really have time."

She said she'd take care of it. The switchboard operator's red mouth was still flirting with the little microphone. With one hand she shoved it aside and looked up at a man in a pair of faded jeans and a short, light-colored windbreaker who was leaning toward her. Her red mouth answered and her hand pointed over to my booth. The man's face was young, clean-shaven, and friendly.

"Helle, this is getting expensive. Say hi to the kids, give them a kiss and a hug, and I'll call you back tomorrow."

"There's a whole lot in the papers today."

"About what?" Now he had turned toward me. He pressed his back against the counter. The switchboard operator's mouth had returned to its silent love-game with the microphone.

"About Charlotte, naturally. Are you really all right, Poul?"

"Of course I am. But you know how I hate to travel." The man pulled a newspaper out of his pocket. He took a couple of steps along the counter so he could lean one shoulder against the wall while pressing his back against the edge of the counter. He was apparently in no hurry.

"You take care of yourself, Poul!"

The man calmly turned a page. He folded up the paper for a moment, holding it in one hand as he lit a cigarette with a cheap disposable lighter.

"Yes, I will. Say hello to everybody."

"Love you. Bye."

As soon as she hung up, I began to tap on the receiver button. The red mouth turned toward me for a moment and in my ear I heard it ask: "*¿Sí?*" The man was still engrossed in his paper. I asked for room 567. She told me to use the lobby telephone.

"Just for a minute," I pleaded. He turned the page and looked up at me. I shaped my lips in soundless Danish words.

"You must use the lobby phone please, sir."

"It's just for a second. For a message. Please connect me."

"OK, why not?"

There was a click, and again a surly "Hello." But this time I told him who I was. Claes remembered me, and before I said another word, he said, "Well, so you want to drive with me after all, my friend?"

"Can you come down here right now? I'm standing by the switchboard, in one of the booths."

"Come on up to my room."

"It's better if you come down here."

"Yeah, but I can't. I've got to take a shower, I'm hung over, and there's a girl here I've got to get rid of right away. My breakfast is on its way up, and my paper just came. I'm not coming downstairs. Come on up to my room in five minutes. See you then!" He hung up.

I did too. I stood there for a minute and then stepped out of the booth. The young man looked up from his paper, stubbed out his cigarette, carefully folded the paper, and stuck it under his arm. Then he came over to me. He walked right past me, straight into the booth, without saying a word.

I got the bill and paid at the counter. I lit another cigarette on my way up in the elevator. A young girl in an orange blouse and turquoise linen pants stepped in as I got out. She smiled and I smiled back.

The door was open so I went right in. I could hear the shower running. I heaved a pile of newspapers out of an easy chair and sat down to wait for him to get out of the shower. While I smoked I tried to figure out what was really wrong with me and why I was so upset.

Charlotte had often wondered why a man with my over-blown imagination and tendency to daydream would choose such a boring field as law. She had also wondered why I didn't make a career as a defense attorney instead of reconciling Common Market regulations in a dusty ministry. Whenever I was mad at her, and that was often, I would yell that one reason I hadn't made a career of it was because I had followed her and encouraged her and accepted that her career was more important. Whenever I was feeling apathetic and slightly depressed I told her I had chosen law because it was easy if you just wanted to get by. And whenever we were close and feeling good about each other — for instance, after we had just made love — I would tell her that, just like everything else in my life, I hadn't chosen law; law had chosen me. And that the discipline of law — the very act of observing the letter of the law and inter-preting it based on established principles — helped keep the demons at a distance. Every once in a while we were able to talk to each other like that. She said many times: Dear, what would you say if I really put on the pressure at the station and got permission to cover a story in Timbuktu, or on the moon, or wherever. It's extremely important, after all.

That was her job — I understood that. But she ran away from responsibility, as usual, claiming to be a slave to her work and an imaginary restlessness. As if she couldn't pick and choose.

Is it any wonder that I found peace in regularity, order, and the perfectionism of trivial things? Calm, cleanliness, and stability are supposed to be what little children need in order to thrive. I do too. Once in a while I would clean out my system by really tying one on, so that dark shadows would dance in my mind for days afterwards. I was 34 and had lived a lifetime. I was 34 years old and had never lived. I saw phantoms on the streets. Imaginary events and people emerged from my dreams and became part of a reality that only I recognized, that only existed in my mind—but sometimes I caught myself trying to share them with other people, as if these ghosts were flesh and blood and not just mirages from my own inner universe.

Why did I get so upset? Why am I the way I am? Or, more precisely in this connection: Why was I the way I was?

"Goddamn, you're a sad-looking Dane!"

Claes Hylander was a very big man. He was standing in the doorway, steaming from the shower, with a towel around his waist, broad-shouldered and sleek, his skin blotched red from the heat. He was briskly rubbing his short hair with another towel.

"Why are you looking so sad this morning? Got a hangover? Carpenters pounding in your brain, as you Danes say? There's a good Danish remedy for that. There on the table. Gammel Dansk bitters. Under the table: two glasses. Pour! Let's drink to last night. A wild evening followed by a wild night. Did you see her on the way in? Orange blouse, brown eyes. Luscious, as you say in Danish. Beautiful. Ah, those sweet-smelling little Spanish pussies. Isn't that what you call them in Denmark?"

He went on in the same vein, like a waterfall. The blue of his eyes was rimmed with fine red lines. In spite of the shower and deodorant he stank of booze, smoke, and bars; decay was visible in his body when he bent over to pick up the lighter from the floor. His stomach crept out of the towel and the fat bulged under his skin. He poured a generous amount of bitters into two glasses.

"Skål!" I said. The drink helped.

Unembarrassed, he threw off the towel and started to get dressed as he continued to talk about his carousing in Madrid's nightlife. About how he had picked up the girl at one in the morning. What they had had to drink. About their screwing. His member was surprisingly little for such a big body. It looked red and used. That pleased me. I sat there like some kind of yokel, gloating, while he pulled on a pair of dark linen pants and a light shirt. Then he sat down on the edge of the bed and poured a couple more shots into the glasses.

"Why are you looking so sad?" he asked.

I told him that it had been an idiotic morning. That I'd gotten some information from Denmark that I didn't under-stand. "I have to call up the Danish embassy. Do you know when they open? I must have gotten his name wrong for some reason. I have to admit I don't really see what the misunder-standing was," I said disjointedly.

He was suddenly quite serious.

"I don't either, my friend. I don't either. As Thor is my witness! You see, I called a friend at the Danish embassy this morning. And he didn't know anyone named Lars Hansen. On the other hand, my friend knows Mr. Simonsen quite well — the man who waited at the airport in vain for a Danish jurist, whose wife had been blown up and who was supposed to arrive in the Spanish capital. But he wasn't even on the plane! Aha, I thought. You're hung over. You've gotten the name wrong. Nope. Lars Hansen doesn't exist."

I took a gulp of the lukewarm liquor. I was feeling much better. I told him about my conversation with Helle.

Claes stared at me with his red eyes.

"Who the hell is he, then?" he asked. "We saw him ourselves. What's going on? Who would show up at the airport and
pass himself off as an official from the Danish embassy, speaking
perfect Danish? How did he even know that you were coming?
Who is he?"

Claes was asking a lot of questions. I asked one too. Unfortunately, and quite typically for me, it wasn't asked for the sake
of clarification; it was a question that reflected what Charlotte
called my dependency syndrome. A fancy phrase for my lack of
independence, as she saw it. I hadn't wanted to be a martyr in
our relationship, so I had seldom protested.

To Claes I said: "So what are we going to do now?"

6

The countryside was bare. There were no trees. Boulders were strewn over the grayish dust. The sky stretched cloudless and vast above the billboards that lined the road. The traffic was heavy, and on the horizon we saw the silhouette of a wooden bull advertising brandy. Trucks belched their way through the desolate landscape.

Claes and I set out alone. He said that his photographer had been called away to some assassination in the Middle East.

He drove fast and confidently. It was only when we were in the car that I realized I hadn't had anything for breakfast except that large coffee with milk and a couple of bottles of mineral water. My hangover was heavy now — it felt sticky and greasy. It sat throbbing at the base of my skull.

We had been in a hurry. Claes packed while he gulped a few mouthfuls of his breakfast. His movements were quick and sure, like someone who has packed his bags many times in his life.

Down in the lobby I thought I caught a glimpse of the man in the light jacket who had been standing outside the booth when I made my call. I tugged at Claes' sleeve, but like a shadow on the wall the man was gone, and Claes gave me a quizzical look.

Back at my hotel, I packed quickly while Claes questioned the clerk at the front desk, who knew nothing about the man from the embassy. He hadn't been at the hotel this morning. No, no one had called for the Danish gentleman. No, the hotel didn't know who he was, had never seen him before. In the little

safe deposit box where I had put my money and ticket to Copenhagen, there was also the plane ticket to San Sebastián. Claes
showed me that it was paid for in cash, but I was the one who
discovered that it was issued on the very day that Charlotte was
blown up. Amazingly fast—before they even knew whether I
was going to come. Claes was skeptical, but had to agree it was
unusual. He shook his head and tried again to drag some information out of the front desk clerk, who smiled—and said he
was sorry.

Finally we gave up, threw the suitcases in the back of the
car, and drove out of the city at breakneck speed. I had taken
along the plane ticket to San Sebastián in my bag. At Claes'
request I had called the Danish embassy. They gave me the
telephone number of the consulate in San Sebastián. I got the
friendly woman to promise that the embassy wouldn't say anything to the Danish reporters, because she said that several
newspapers had already called to find out where they could
reach me.

We took turns driving, which gave me childish pleasure.
Claes propped his long legs up on the dashboard, with the seat
pushed all the way back and a can of beer in his hand, and told
me stories from his many travels. He was quiet, calm, and
matter-of-fact. This was a different side of his temperament.
The professional in him. The side I preferred to the playboy.
But strangely enough he wouldn't talk about Charlotte, about
the "incident," as I called it in my mind. He refused to talk
about it, grumbled and seemed uneasy. He got me to stop the
car so he could make a phone call, but didn't say who he was
calling. Maybe he knew something, but he didn't tell me a
thing. I prodded him a couple of times and got the cold
shoulder.

We ate lunch in a café by the roadside with loud men in blue
overalls who were eating mountains of food. We picked at our

food and paid more attention to the wine. Claes seemed to be going around with something inside him that he couldn't or wouldn't let out. He made several more calls and each time came back from the telephone with an even more concerned expression.

I withdrew into myself, searching for my grief for Charlotte. I felt sad, but did I feel any grief? The greatest sorrow on earth is losing the one you love — or something like that. But did I feel that way? Only if one of my kids died. But wouldn't I repress it the way I tended to repress everything else, push it away, hide it in the very back of my mind? I often felt like I was living in a bell jar. As if the multitude of horrors in the surrounding world just bounced off me, as if they were taking place on the other side of the glass without concerning me directly, without touching me. Was I incapable of feeling pain, joy, anger, hatred? Or could I only drift with the current? — floating calmly along while I warded off all conflicts by slipping away from them like a half-back slips out of a tackle.

Questions and more questions, and no answers. Late in the afternoon Claes woke up and I told him that there had been a red Opel on our tail. A coincidence, he said, and withdrew into his shell when he took over the wheel.

Finally I gave up and fell asleep.

When I woke up we had turned off the highway and he had slowed down drastically. A red light was shining in front of us, swinging slowly back and forth. A green Land Rover, parked by the side of the road, was visible in the yellow glow of the streetlights.

"What's all this?" I asked.

Claes slowed down and put on his turn signal.

"*Guardia civil.* Roadblock. There are lots of them here in Basque country. Get out your passport."

He pulled over to the side of the road.

"What would happen if you didn't stop?"

"They'd shoot. And they don't fire a warning shot first. They'd be within the law too, my friend. A ruling from 1942 that gives them permission to shoot if you don't stop your car immediately when they signal."

"Yes, but they were waiting right by a corner. What if we hadn't seen them?"

"A few people die that way every year."

Claes rolled down his window. An officer in an olive-green uniform with a pistol at his belt came over to the car.

I had expected him to have on the typical patent leather hat of the *guardia civil*, but he was wearing a military cap. He looked like a soldier. A second officer placed himself in front of the car, and when I turned halfway around I saw a third one take up a position behind the car. Both were armed with snub-nosed submachine guns. Over by the Land Rover there were two more officers, also with submachine guns, and two additional Land Rovers were parked in the dark. The windows were barred.

"Buenas noches. Documentación, ¡por favor!" he said politely in a low monotone.

Claes took my passport and handed it to him with his own.

"Ah, foreigners. Do you speak Spanish?"

"I speak Spanish, *señor*. Can we help you with anything?"

"And excellent Spanish at that. Our apologies. This is simply routine. Do you have papers for the car?"

Claes reached across me. He had to unfasten his seat belt so he could manage to rummage in the glove compartment for the folder from the car rental agency. He handed this out the window too. I noticed how the officer took a small step back as soon as Claes started to search for the papers. Was he stepping out of the line of fire? At any rate, I understood what Claes had meant when he said earlier that things were deadly serious in Basque country. I had never lived in a country under terror, so like most Danes I had a somewhat romantic and hazy idea of what that entails. On film and in the papers it doesn't seem nearly as spooky as it felt to me during this routine investigation. No one had ever pointed a loaded weapon at me before. I was nervous and had a guilty conscience even though there was, of course, no reason for me to feel guilty.

"A rental car, I see," said the officer. "Are you in Spain on vacation or on business?"

"Business," said Claes. "We're on our way to San Sebastián from Madrid."

"Would you please get out of the car and open the trunk? I'm sorry, but it's my duty. Not everyone here in Spain understands how to live together in a democratic way, as I'm sure you know. It's merely routine."

Again he took a few steps back. I unfastened my seat belt. About twenty yards away another car was waved over to the side. I had started to sweat. Were the submachine guns' safeties on or off? Couldn't the guns easily go off by mistake? I was so nervous that I almost didn't see the red Opel whiz past. The *guardia civil* didn't give it a second glance. Claes didn't seem nervous at all, just annoyed at the inconvenience. I got out and was immediately overwhelmed with a great urge to take a piss. The air tasted of pine forests and spring rain; it smelled clean and cool after the heavy tobacco smoke in the car.

Claes went around and unlocked the trunk. I wondered if they were going to frisk us too. How do you really react to that? Do you position yourself with legs spread and hands planted on the roof of the car while strong hands pat down your body with great expertise? Not only had no one ever pointed a loaded gun at me before; I realized that I had never been threatened physically in any way since I got out of school. In spite of all the newspaper reports about the increase in violence in Denmark, I had never been bothered, either at night or during the day.

I could only dimly remember my last fight, on the playground when I was ten years old — a punch in the nose and the mixture of blood, snot, and tears that poured down my face.

The officer cast an indifferent glance into the trunk and handed the passports back to Claes, who shut the trunk and locked it. The officer saluted and went back to the Land Rover with his colleagues. We got in the car and drove off.

"What a damn hassle," said Claes, lighting a cigarette.

"Does this happen a lot in Spain these days, in a democracy?"

"Not in Spain so much, but in Basque country it's pretty much a daily occurrence."

"I don't like the sight of machine guns pointed at innocent people."

"They don't like seeing their buddies with blood spouting out of holes made by the ETA's bullets, either."

We didn't talk after that. We were getting closer to San Sebastián. You could see the glow in the sky up ahead; from the highway, up in the hills, the first suburbs were visible. In the yellow artificial light, billowing clouds of steam danced from factory smokestacks and from other pipes, tubes, holes, and cracks. It was as if the factories were leaking all over, and the air tasted like sulfur.

"This is nothing compared to Bilbao," said Claes. "We'll take a little detour. We're driving through Rentería now, a working-class suburb. It's San Sebastián's Liverpool, gray and filthy. It's near the French border."

"Why the detour?"

"To see whether our friends in the red Opel are still following us."

"Are they?" I asked, thinking: He takes me seriously after all.

"I haven't seen a trace of them since the roadblock."

He swore and shifted down. By now we had left the four-lane highway far behind and were driving past dreary gray housing projects. The traffic wasn't heavy; there was a red light shining up ahead again, but this time they let us drive past. Again I saw three green Land Rovers with barred windows and silent officers armed with automatic rifles glowering into the evening darkness. Farther in toward the center of town we saw another roadblock. This time the officers had brown uniforms and, besides the two Land Rovers, the checkpoint had a jeep and a grayish-white armored truck, which I just caught a glimpse of as we were waved through.

"Am I seeing things . . . was that a tank?"

"It sure was — with a gun turret, water cannon, and everything."

"Is it always like this?"

"No, but the ETA shot a policeman this morning, here in Rentería, so they're looking for explosives."

"Why explosives?"

"The ETA stole over 500 kilos of plastic explosives a week ago from an ammunition plant near Pamplona. The Basque country is full of ammunition plants."

"Five hundred kilos! What are they thinking of using it for?"

"That's why there are rumors of some big action coming up. To show the shitheads in Madrid that the organization still packs a punch."

"Rumors?"

"Only rumors."

The buildings were nicer-looking now, and there were people on the streets. They were almost all dressed in carnival costumes. Even though it was nearly 9 o'clock, there were swarms of children in smocks, masks, dresses, and colorful costumes, holding little shepherd's crooks in their hands, with their faces painted in bright colors.

"It's the next to last night of Carnival," said Claes. "Then tomorrow is the Sardine's funeral."

"And what's that?"

"You'll see for yourself." Again that aloof brush-off, as if the carnival were some big state secret.

We drove over a bridge. Now the traffic was heavy. Pedestrians came from both directions in a constant stream; many were in costume, and those that weren't looked like they spent a lot of money on clothes. They looked more French than Spanish, I thought.

Claes swung to the left and ahead of us was the ocean, behind a promenade with bare trees and globe lamps on ornate dark green posts. The sidewalk tiles shone white in spite of the evening darkness. It was swarming with people, and through the rolled-down window I could hear the waves slowly rolling in to the beach. It was very beautiful.

"Can you afford 400 kroner for a hotel room?" Claes asked.

"That's a lot."

"We'll find another one for you, but I'm going to stay here. At the newspaper's expense, of course."

He pointed to a massive white building right in front of us that reached all the way out to the promenade, like a steamer that was ready to put out to sea across the bay.

We drove back the way we had come, but this time a little higher up, and a few hundred yards down the road Claes stopped the car in front of a little hotel built into the side of the hill. It was just four stories high and looked rather decrepit with its peeling ochre-colored paint, but the balconies faced the bay. As we got out of the car, I could see there was an island in the middle of the bay.

The front desk was on the second floor. A middle-aged woman in a blue sweater with a red pattern was standing behind the counter. You could hear a TV from the next room. The lobby was very tiny, with two armchairs, a poster showing the bay in sunshine, and a little stand with postcards that looked yellow and lost, as if they had given up and no longer believed a tourist would ever come by.

The air was cold and a little damp. I felt a gray melancholy, and my legs wouldn't really work right after so many hours in the car. The woman smiled when she saw Claes, who was carrying my suitcase while I clutched my small flight bag in my left hand.

" ¡Hola!" she said happily and let herself be kissed on both cheeks. Claes had to lean way over to reach her face. I stood in the background and made do with a nod.

Claes turned around. "It's cheap, clean, and comfortable. I always stay here when I'm on my own."

"It looks fine. And just for a couple of nights," I said.

My bladder was about to explode, so the sooner the formalities were over with the better. The woman stared with that attentive, blank expression people get when they don't understand what's being said, even though the conversation may concern them personally.

"It looks very nice here. I only need the room for two nights," I said slowly in Spanish.

Her face brightened.

"Oh, you speak such good Spanish."

She handed me a little yellow card and asked me to sign it and to turn in my passport.

"312, señor," she said, giving me the key. I understood that I had to carry my suitcase up myself. That was nice. I can't stand being waited on by other people. Claes pushed the button for the elevator, and it started down toward us, creaking and wheezing.

"Do you want to come over to my hotel when you're done? You know, the big white one we drove past. It's called Hotel Londres. It's just a five-minute walk from here."

"Shall we say in about an hour?" I asked.

"That's about right. We can meet in the bar."

The elevator landed with a bump. There was just room enough for the suitcases and one person. It was the kind where you squirm like an eel to push back the last sliding door and hold it open while you struggle to squeeze yourself, your bags, and your suitcase in all at the same time. I made it and saw Claes turn on his heel and disappear just as the door closed. I immediately felt depressed at the thought of being alone again, far from home in a country whose language I could barely speak.

The room was little and dark with a double bed in the middle of the floor and a picture of a saint on the wall, but when I opened the shutters the salt air streamed in from the sea and the light of the moon cut a swath in the calm gray ocean, and I could hear the slow, heavy rhythm of the surf.

The bathroom was small too, but the water was hot, and I stood under the shower for a long time with an empty bladder. Then I picked up the old-fashioned black telephone and asked the woman at the front desk to connect me with the number in San Sebastián that I had gotten from the Danish embassy in Madrid.

A woman's voice answered. In my halting Spanish I explained who I was. Three times she repeated that the consul wasn't home that evening but that he was expecting me at his office the next day, no later than 11 o'clock. Did I have the consul's address? The consul also sent his deepest sympathy. Would I please give her my address in San Sebastián?

I got out the card with the room number on it. It had the price, the address, and the telephone number listed.

"Hotel Ixtas Gain," I said.

I repeated it a few minutes later when I got a connection through to Helle miraculously fast. I gave her the phone number too, and she promised to send a telex to the Danish embassy in Madrid when she got to work in the morning.

It was a good connection.

"The pack is on its way," she said.

"What did you say?"

"I said the hounds are on the loose. The story has been out for hours, and now the reporters know that you've gone down there to get Charlotte . . . Charlotte's body. So now the so-called yellow press is on its way. Charlotte was a big name in Denmark, you know."

"Yeah, I know. But I don't want to have anything to do with them."

"They could be in San Sebastián by tomorrow," she said, unimpressed. "Try to see it from their angle. It's a good story, you know."

Helle is an extremely sensible member of the human race, but she's just as thick-headed as most other journalists when it comes to their mythical god: the good story.

"I don't want to have anything to do with them," I repeated. I suddenly got a nasty suspicion. "You're not the one who turned them loose on me, are you?"

"Come off it, Poul. How can you even think that?"

"You always owe each other for some damn thing."

"Poul! Cut it out, will you."

I wasn't convinced, but I had heard that the kids were fine, so I guessed there wasn't much more to say.

"If I'm lucky I should be able to leave here tomorrow," I said. "You can tell that to your drooling hounds. It's not worth their while to come down here. They can wait for me at Copenhagen Airport."

"Poul, you're being unfair. I haven't said a thing to anyone — where you are or what your plans are. What are they, by the way?"

"To come home with Charlotte as soon as possible. I'll call you when I know more. Goodbye."

I hung up on her protests and regretted that I'd given her the

name of my hotel. But as I got dressed — gray slacks, a light
sweater over a beige shirt, and my tweed jacket — some of my
anger evaporated. After all, she was taking care of my kids. And
if anything happened to them she had to be able to get hold of
me. Besides, I would have even more use for her in the future
when I had to get serious about starting a life for myself alone
with the kids. I hadn't even had a chance to think about it yet.
What about the future? I had to see about finding another job at
least. My part-time salary would last about as long as a snowball
in hell. It wouldn't even cover the payments on the apartment.

I had taken the stairs down, and my train of thought was
interrupted by the woman at the front desk when I put my key
on the counter.

"Excuse me, *señor*," she said, putting her hand on my arm.
"Your friend told me about your wife. About the tragedy in the
bar. I'm very sorry. God rest her soul." She crossed herself.

"She isn't the only one. Many people die here in the Basque
country."

She said something quickly, something I didn't understand.
Then she repeated slowly, "Things like that happen in an occupied country."

"Occupied?" I said.

"Euskadi is occupied by Spain. We aren't free here. Yet."
Her eyes glowed.

"*Adiós*," I said without further comment.

"*Agurr*," she said in Basque.

It was cool outside, but the air was fresh. I cut across the
road and walked along the promenade toward the big white
hotel, which I could see a few hundred yards down toward the
town. The waves were lapping almost all the way up to the
vertical granite wall. The bay was formed by two promontories
with an island like a black blob a little to the right of one
of them. A beautiful natural harbor. High up on one of the

promontories you could see a big cross, or was it a statue of Christ? The crowds on the promenade had thinned out considerably. Mostly young, costumed carnival revelers were now making their way toward town in groups, arm in arm.

I turned to the future again. Especially the financial side. You could say a lot of different things about Charlotte, but she had been a good provider. There was her steady salary at the radio and TV station, as well as income from articles in Danish and Scandinavian newspapers. She had written books and had sat on a couple of commissions for national security and foreign policy. There was money from that too. We had gotten used to a very comfortable standard of living.

It wasn't until I reached the Hotel Londres and was looking for the entrance that I realized I was now, of course, a rich man. In fact I was worth over a million kroner. There was Charlotte's group life insurance through the union, in addition to a life insurance policy that we'd taken out ourselves. And as part of her pension plan, Charlotte had some accumulated capital in the bank. Her publisher had also taken out travel and accident insurance on her. There's money for the kids, too, I thought as I pushed my way through the swinging door into the hotel's comfortable carpeted lobby with soft chairs and sofas, crystal chandeliers, and that quiet calm which apparently goes along with wealth. I asked the way to the bar. Actually I could have afforded to stay there myself, but I just didn't have the energy to move.

Claes, newly shaven, was sitting with a red drink in front of him, next to a guy in his mid-thirties with short hair, who was looking straight at me and who looked like a very good midfielder on a professional soccer team.

In his pan-Scandinavian, Claes said, "Come and meet one of my friends from town. He's promised to show us the bar, or the remains of it, where Charlotte was blown up."

What was I supposed to say? Thanks a lot? The Basque
solved the problem by putting out his hand and pressing mine
firmly for a long time, as he looked straight into my eyes.

" *¡Hola!* I'm very sorry. She was a very special woman."

His eyes weren't really brown. They were practically black,
and they seemed much older than the handsome Latin face with
the regular features. I was quite sure that I was staring into the
eyes of Charlotte's Basque lover.

7

*I*t was a soot-blackened hole in the midst of the colorful carnival, which was in full swing all around us.

A black hole, scantily screened off with cardboard and sheets of plywood. A gaping cavity in the row of houses. With soot-covered, twisted fixtures scattered all over. On the walls were the remains of posters and lamps. A loudspeaker hung by its cord as if balancing on the edge of an abyss. The ceiling had been shoddily propped up. The zinc counter was surprisingly beautiful, like an abstract, futuristic painting, shining with all the colors of the rainbow. There was a stench of soot, mutilation, and unnecessary death.

So this is where she died. In a thousandth of a second, without knowing what hit her. The bomb had been placed in a handbag in the bathroom, which was in the back of the bar, up against a heavy firewall. Which meant that the full force of the explosion had been channeled outward. Furniture and human bodies were flung through the swinging doors, now torn off, and out into the street, into the wall across the way.

There was no trace left in the street. The corpses had been carted away. The furniture had been tossed into the remains of the bar. Small groups from the carnival processions passed by singing, as if a bombing in San Sebastián were nothing unusual.

And there was no trace of her.

I walked around in the bar alone; the others waited discreetly outside on the street. I don't know what I was searching for. A memento, perhaps. A torn-off button, a scrap of her handbag, a page from her cursed notebook that she was always scribbling in instead of living in the present with me and the kids — who were her kids too.

There was nothing. The floor was covered with ashes and cold embers, still steaming from the water of the firehoses. There were shards of glass everywhere, scraps of labels from liquor bottles, disintegrated, unrecognizable pieces of furniture, and a lump of meat almost turned to charcoal. It lay jammed into a corner, partially covered by a one-legged stool and a little table that once had green tiles on it. For a moment I thought the rescue squad had overlooked it. I was filled with horror; besides the smell of wet ashes there was the smell of burned meat, like the pork roast my mother forgot in the oven when I was thirteen years old. My stomach turned over and exploded its contents over the stinking meat, which I now saw was not only in the corner but in several places, in chunks of various sizes.

Claes took my arm. He was leading me out, but I pulled free and pointed. Claes turned pale too, but then he suddenly started to laugh. I was still gasping for air, and I belched from way down in my stomach; it took a while for me to understand what he was saying. When it finally sank in, I also started laughing uncontrollably, almost insanely. I remembered that Spanish cafés always had big smoked hams hanging in row after row over the bar, ready to slice for the hungry customer.

Laughing, we came out onto the street, where a group of inebriated, costumed young people pulled us into their circle and dragged us around in a drunken, uproarious dance — around and around until I could only see Claes' wide-open eyes and laughing mouth and the dancers' painted faces and cartoon masks, going around and around, wilder and wilder, faster and faster, and getting blurrier all the time until finally everything turned completely and totally black.

I was only out for a moment. Later I learned that Miguel had grabbed me when I fell. He was supporting my head when I

came to, propped up against a wall. No one gave me a second
look. Just another drunk at the carnival this year. The first thing
I noticed was the sound of the carnival. It wasn't imported
samba, but something else. Brutal drums in a heavy, pumping
rhythm, screaming horns, and flutes that sounded like bagpipes,
and then the drums again, which were not Spanish or Latin but
came out of the depths of the past. I stared into Miguel's eyes,
which seemed to be saying, curious yet sympathetic, that this
was just the beginning of something much worse.

The thudding drums followed us through the narrow streets,
empty of cars, over to a little table in a restaurant in the old part
of town. I splashed some water on my face, combed my hair,
and got rid of some of the worst spots on my clothes, still in a
daze, as if I were watching someone else going through the
motions. I reeked of soot and wet ashes and a faint stink of
vomit, but finally I was sitting there with a menu in my hand,
with water and wine in glasses in front of me. And I felt relieved,
empty, and confused all at the same time. Claes was working on
a gin and tonic—his third? Miguel was drinking water and a
little wine.

Miguel Uribe Boyer—that's how he had introduced himself
in a monotone in the bar of the Hotel Londres.

"Miguel is my friend," Claes had said. But was that true?
Miguel treated Claes politely and cordially—but without
warmth. Miguel called him by his first name even though his
tone of voice seemed to require a more formal title. They acted
as though they knew each other in the way a journalist knows a
very good source. Mutual dependence does not necessarily lead
to friendship.

Miguel was obviously a familiar face in the restaurant.
Everybody knew him—and not only the waitresses; he had also
said hello to many people in the room, which was a little like a
German *Bierstube*. People of many generations sat at the tables

eating in almost reverent silence, even those in carnival costume who were there resting up to go back to the dance.

Food is one of my weaknesses — cooking it as well as eating
it. With two small children I seldom get to a restaurant. Normally I wouldn't feel comfortable in a restaurant in a foreign
country with someone I didn't really know, but that evening I
felt fine, almost in protest. I looked at Miguel's squarish face,
his short stiff hair, his five-o'clock shadow, and his black eyes.
Why did I have the feeling that he had been Charlotte's lover —
or maybe even more than that, her beloved?

Miguel raised his head and locked his eyes with mine for a
moment.

"What are you thinking about?" he asked in the slow Spanish he made a special effort to speak with me. But strangely
enough it sounded as though he spoke Spanish with an accent.

"I'm wondering what you do," I said.

"What I do? A little of everything. I write, and I'm the editor
of a journal."

"A quasi-communist, nationalistic propaganda magazine,"
Claes interrupted in his nearly perfect Spanish spoken with a
Swedish accent. His eyes were getting red and swollen, and his
second face was starting to appear. I was getting to know him.
There were two versions of Claes — one sober, the other drunk.

"Why don't you tell him a little about your past, you murderer," Claes continued with a smile that didn't completely hide
the undercurrent of anger in his voice.

Miguel just smiled and let his eyes sweep over Claes' face for
a moment.

"You tell him. Then I can concentrate on the menu."

I looked up at Claes. There was a tension between them that
I couldn't explain. Maybe I was being overly sensitive, tired after
emptying my stomach. I was still feeling dazed. It hadn't sunk in
that I was sitting here wifeless, almost a millionaire, a single

father, and alone with two unknown figures in a foreign country
in an unfamiliar town inhabited by drunken people in costume.

I looked inquiringly at Claes, who drained his gin and tonic
and at the same time filled his wine glass to the brim with red
wine. He was sitting to my right; he leaned toward me and
switched over to Swedish. He was businesslike again.

"What do I know? Miguel was one of the organization's
leaders during Franco's rule and up until 1977. I don't know
exactly what he did, but I bet he had his hand in kidnappings,
bank robberies, maybe murder. You can't tell by the way a man
looks whether he has killed for the sake of the cause. He himself
only admits to being a member and to helping plan a large-scale
escape from a prison down near Segovia in 1976. They dug a
tunnel and more than thirty men escaped through the sewer
system. The *guardia civil* caught all of them again."

"Oh, so he's been in prison too." We both took another sip
of red wine.

"Yes, for almost three years. As you can see, he's a little
cautious with the wine. He was brutally tortured at the *guardia
civil*'s station here in town and at the headquarters of the Security Police in Madrid. It damaged his kidneys, and I don't know
what it did to him psychologically. He never talks about it."

"That big red building at Puerta del Sol?" I asked.

"Yeah, that's the one. But why do you ask?"

"No reason in particular. I was thinking about something
the mysterious man from the Danish embassy said to me about
that place, but now I can't remember what it was."

We took another sip.

"I interrupted you. Go on."

"There's not much more to tell. In 1977, when Spain was
going to hold its first elections since 1936, the government was
stuck with a real hot potato: the ETA prisoners. The government
wanted to give some sort of amnesty to all political prisoners, but

they knew the armed forces would be furious if they turned loose
that bunch of nationalistic murderers. So they sent them out of
the country until the elections were over."

"Where to?"

"Different places. Miguel was one of the four that Denmark
agreed to accept. Ask him if he can say 'Helsingør'."

Miguel looked up when he heard the name of the town. He
smiled broadly so his whole melancholy face lit up. Only his
eyes remained dead. God knows what they had done to him at
the police station. My knowledge of these matters stemmed from
reports about prisoners of the Gestapo and atavistic Latin
American regimes, but this was Europe in the 1970s we were
talking about, after all. Weren't they exaggerating?

I was about to ask him about Denmark, but then we had to
order. Salad, vegetable soup, and sole meunière for everyone.
And some more wine.

In Danish I said to Claes, "What about after 1977?"

"You mean is he still a member of the organization?"

"Uh-huh."

Claes looked like he was weighing the question.

"No, I don't think so. He has said goodbye to weapons. He
supports the movement toward autonomy that's under way, but
on the basis of the constitution, as it were."

"So what does he have to say about terrorism today?"

"He's against it. He thinks it's politically unjustifiable,
pointless, but he will never wholeheartedly call it terrorism."

"What does he call it then?"

"Armed struggle. The Basques don't waste any tears when a
peasant from some godforsaken Andalusian village is shot down
around here. When he puts on a police uniform he becomes
part of the occupation army. You and I look at it morally.
Miguel doesn't." Claes glanced toward Miguel. "For him it's
just no longer politically justifiable, or opportune, if you will."

"But do they still have the support of the people?"

"Support . . . maybe not. But did the Danes who disapproved of sabotage against the occupation forces report people to the Germans during World War II?"

"No, I guess not."

"Why not?" Claes asked.

"How should I know? For patriotic reasons or out of fear of reprisals, I would think."

"It's the same thing here."

"But Miguel has done all right?"

"Yes, he has, and in his own backhanded way he's probably one of the most loyal servants the present democratic state can find, even though Miguel would probably rather swallow that bottle than admit it. Thank God, here comes the food at last!"

It was the soup, steaming, thick with peas, beans, carrots, and other vegetables, and there was fresh-baked bread with a crunchy crust. We ate in reverent silence. It wasn't until all three of us had sopped up the last of the soup with some bread that I asked Miguel:

"Do you know Charlotte from Denmark?" My faulty knowledge of the Spanish language made my question bring her back to the ranks of the living, and the formulation of the question made the loss of her break open inside me. I knew that I would miss her. I was suddenly sure of that. Her body, her soul, her presence as an essential part of my life. It's possible that my grief had a touch of sentimentality, helped along by the wine, but the feeling was genuine enough at the moment. My voice shook when I repeated the question to Miguel, who looked as if he either hadn't understood it the first time or was very surprised by it.

"Do you know Charlotte from Denmark?" he repeated, astonished. He pronounced Charlotte without the final "e."

"Yes, pardon my bad Spanish."

"No, it's excellent. I met Charlotte several times in Denmark. She interviewed us. She saw to it that we met some people and got around a bit after all those years in prison."

Claes was staring at him with a smirk. Were the three of us sitting there sharing the memory of Charlotte's body? I said that Miguel had mentioned earlier that he thought Charlotte was a very special woman. Dinner guests were still coming into the restaurant. In Denmark I would be on my way to bed by now. Our waitress came by and said that the fish was just about done. She had beads of sweat in the short blond hairs on her upper lip. Claes was looking at her with undisguised admiration. The carnival guests in the corner were starting to liven up as more bottles of wine were put on the table. One of them was dressed like a pirate. He had put his fake iron hook on the tablecloth next to him. His shirtfront was blotched with wine; it matched the whites of his eyes.

"Special. That's right." Miguel slowly exhaled the black, pungent smoke from his Ducados cigarette toward me. Once again there was an intensity in his expression — this time even in his black eyes, although they still looked like they bore a deep sorrow. Along his jaw on the left side there was a row of small scars. "We called her La Danesa. We can't really pronounce 'Charlotte.' Everyone on the political scene here knows her. She has been coming to Euskadi for years, you know."

He drank a little mineral water and took another deep drag on the cigarette so the small scars shone white against his dark complexion.

"Am I talking too fast?" he asked.

"No, but what is Euskadi?"

He looked at me ironically.

"The Basque country is called Euskadi. That's the name of our fatherland, just as your fatherland is Denmark."

"Fatherland sounds a little — how do you say — *altmodisch*."

Miguel looked a little disoriented. To my surprise, Claes had been listening. He knew I didn't know the Spanish word for "old-fashioned" and said it in Spanish to Miguel.

"That's because you take yours for granted," said Miguel. His voice had become hard, metallic. "Would you accept being under German rule?"

"No, we wouldn't."

"Well, why should we accept being under Spanish rule? Why should we accept Madrid determining our future? Why can't we have a decolonization?"

Political discussions everywhere. At home and in Spain. In our crowd, thank God, they were being replaced by subjects like jogging, food, morals, relationships, religion, and therapy — which are, after all, more interesting. At any rate I hadn't intended to get involved in an academic debate about nationalism in the Basque country. It was none of my business. The only reason I was in the Basque country — Euskadi — was to claim my wife's body. Charlotte had been professionally involved. I arrogantly decided that I didn't want to get involved in any way . . . other than eating their no doubt excellent sole.

So I smiled my evasive, understanding smile and turned the palms of my hands toward Miguel in a gesture that could mean both surrender and an apology for my linguistic shortcomings.

But Miguel still looked angry, so Poul Jensen the mediator stepped forward quickly with a new subject.

"The police in Denmark said Charlotte might have been helping the Basques — the ETA?"

Miguel relaxed again.

"Claes told me at the hotel about your shadow and the mysterious man in Madrid from the Danish embassy. It's possible they're from the Security Police — who knows? They're paranoid about anything that has to do with Euskadi."

Now he was looking straight at me. I looked right past him,

fascinated by the pirate's hook that had speared a piece of bread and was victoriously waving its booty in the air. The waitress laughed indulgently at the party, which was getting louder and louder. There was a woman in a clown costume sitting next to the pirate, and she was the one my eyes sought out again. I had caught her several times staring straight at our table. Half of her face was painted blue and the other half white; her body was hidden in the billowing, voluminous clown suit. Her short-cropped hair was more brown than black, and the fine line of her throat glowed above the clown suit's clerical ruff.

"La Danesa wasn't involved," said Miguel after a pause. He followed my glance over to the corner table, smiled, took his glass and raised it with an ironic nod of his head toward the clown girl. She lifted her glass too and replied with a smile that revealed her even white teeth behind the broad, red-painted lips.

The sole came; it was heavenly in fresh sizzling butter, with a plain boiled potato and lemon and sprinkled with fresh parsley. And a new bottle of wine was put on the table. I still hadn't found out why Miguel thought Charlotte was a special kind of woman, but I didn't really care anymore either. I almost didn't even care whether he had been her Basque lover or whether he was a murderer and a terrorist. In short, the wine was starting to have its blissful effect. But my hyper-exhaustion seemed to be preventing me from getting seriously drunk. My head wasn't getting heavy — it felt lighter. My words weren't getting slurred — my Spanish was getting faster and clearer, and unknown words were popping up from my unconscious.

I didn't feel sleepy. Like an animal that can finally shed its winter coat, I shook off the heavy stench from the bombed-out café where the explosion had started this whole process.

The fish knife felt good in my hand, and with small, careful cuts we separated the fine sole meat from the bone. Miguel and I ate slowly and with enjoyment. Claes picked at his food, paying more attention to the bottle, while his eyes darted around the room. The restaurant was sweltering now, and the young waitresses in blue dresses had glowing cheeks. Now it was just as noisy indoors as out, so the clamor of the carnival faded into the background.

I raised my glass to Miguel.

"Why was Charlotte special?"

"Special?"

"Yes, you called her special at the hotel." With a simple gliding motion he turned the fish over and began to loosen the meat, which fell elegantly off the bone. Claes had pushed his plate away and lit another cigarette.

"She was exceptional both as a journalist and as a human being," said Miguel. "Everything is politicized here in Basque country. We are a contentious people. Even the punkers and junkies are in some way involved in spite of their passivity. Political analyses are often inadequate. Here, like everywhere else, they are overshadowed by human foolishness. La Danesa came here to get material from the progressives and the reactionaries, the nationalists and the Spaniards, and she was welcome everywhere."

Had I been married to a saint? I thought. Or had I found here in Basque country a people who were more self-centered than the Danes, who let themselves be duped by a foreigner's interest in their trivial problems?

"She was a journalist," I said as a kind of explanation. "That was her job."

"She was more than that. She was a friend."

"A friend?"

"A friend of many people. She was liked, loved."

"Loved?"

Miguel looked at me astonished. His fork with the piece of fish paused in front of his mouth.

"She was your wife, Poul. She was beautiful and charming. You know that."

"*Una santa!*"

Miguel laughed loudly and, uncharacteristically, slapped me on the shoulder.

"My friend! She was no saint as defined by the holy Roman Catholic church. That she wasn't."

"What do you mean?"

The laughter stopped abruptly.

"That she was a saint by my definition. That she was a great woman. That it was an honor to have known her."

These were un-Danish words. Their grandiloquence embarrassed me a little, even though they seemed less powerful in the foreign language than in Danish. In my internal translation they became rather ridiculous and awkward. They smelled of B-movies and TV shows from the USA.

"You're not saying she was . . ." I searched for the word and found it: ". . . *una puta?*"

Claes just about choked on his cigarette.

"Take it easy, Dane. Take it easy. We were getting along just fine," he said.

Miguel's face turned chalk-white, so white that even the small scars on his jaw disappeared. His knuckles gleamed as he gripped the fork.

"You were married to La Danesa. Otherwise I would have killed you for that word," he said. I had called her a whore. In Spanish it hadn't sounded so bad, but now translated into Danish in my mind, I realized the enormity of what I had said. I also realized that Miguel literally meant what he said. That he wasn't a man who used words as an empty threat, as a figure of

speech. Miguel was the first person I had met who had probably
personally killed another human being. He had taken life. For
him death was not just a movie.

"Forgive me, Miguel," said the husband to the lover who
was defending the unfaithful wife's honor. "The shock, the
grief. . . I don't know what got into me."

Miguel relaxed and Claes inhaled without getting smoke
down the wrong tube this time.

"That's all right."

"I don't know what got into me."

"I said it's OK."

"It's because I loved her so much, and every day I lost a little
more of her."

I didn't know where the words were coming from. The sentence came out in fluent, correct Spanish, as if it had been lying
there all these years, waiting to emerge.

Miguel smiled and his face changed, brightened, so he
looked ten years younger.

"I understand you, my friend."

"I think you actually do."

"I understand you. She was a woman you could possess for a
moment but never own."

In my drunkenness Claes' rolling eyes couldn't disturb the
solidarity, the shared fate, that I felt as I raised my glass to
Miguel, and the husband and lover became one flesh.

"To Charlotte!"

"To La Danesa!"

"Till death do you part," said Claes.

8

And then things began to get lively. Claes continued his efforts to make contact with the waitress. She was short and plump, with big eyes and a mouth that looked like it was perpetually shaped in a question mark. As the evening wore on, Claes' offensive seemed to be working.

Miguel showed a new side of himself. He was funny and entertaining, and he told us about his introduction to Denmark.

One morning in May, a Danish police officer had presented himself to Miguel and three other Basques imprisoned in Burgos. The nice English-speaking officer had with him an official document with the seal of the Danish Crown on it. If they signed the paper they could board a plane to Denmark that very afternoon. To where? To Denmark. Why not? They would sign up for a trip to hell just to get out of the prison in Burgos.

So that afternoon they sat in a plane on their way north to a village outside Helsingør. The Danish Refugee Agency was well-meaning, but they misunderstood the situation. They thought the four men would arrive as human skeletons, debilitated, with sunken cheeks and shaven heads. But in Spanish prisons the political prisoners live well, better than in the French ones, in Miguel's opinion. The beatings in the interrogation rooms are over. The uncertainty is past. The prisoners receive food from their families; they smoke very little and aren't allowed to drink much wine. The days pass with studying and physical training. They leave the prison in a champion boxer's condition.

So Miguel and his comrades didn't want quiet, solitude, and compassion. They wanted crowds of people, taverns, voices, and above all else contact with the opposite sex. They had told this to Charlotte when she interviewed them shortly after they arrived in Denmark.

Charlotte had understood them. And they had immediately put their trust in this small Danish woman. Hadn't I seen that interview?

Laughter rang around the table when, a little haltingly and a little drunk, I explained that because of our young children I didn't always get to watch the Danish evening news, which started at 7:30.

I was pleased with their way of dealing with death — laugh in its face, I thought drunkenly, trying to forget that Charlotte was lying in a cold room not far from where we were drinking.

Suddenly there were a lot of us at the table. The clown girl and her party had joined us with their wine and brandy glasses. She didn't laugh, just smiled, again revealing the even white teeth behind the wide, painted lips. Her hair was cut very short and she had little gold rings in her ears; she had long, strong fingers, which were playing with a disposable lighter decorated with a Basque flag. It looked like the Danish flag. Except there were two diagonal green stripes over the white cross on the red background.

Charlotte had understood the needs of the four men. She had introduced them around, helped them sublet an apartment, soothed the worries of the Refugee Agency, and threatened the Immigration Police with her position. They were an overnight success. The commandos of socialism and freedom, direct from Franco's prisons. The Danish left wing loved them, skin and all. Now I remembered that I'd been to a party with three of them. Miguel hadn't been there that evening.

Then one day they disappeared. After the parliamentary election they left Denmark unnoticed, without notifying the Danish authorities.

Charlotte was the only one they told. She had helped them. Wasn't it reasonable that later they had helped her? She was a brave girl. They owed her a lot. Long live Charlotte and Euskadi!

Our party was the last one in the restaurant. The waiter and one of the waitresses had started putting the chairs up on the tables. But the little plump waitress was now sitting at our table next to Claes with a glass of wine. She had changed from her apron and dress into jeans and a shirt with a blue sweater over it. She had combed her hair into a long ponytail, and the fine drops of sweat had disappeared from her upper lip. She looked very young.

She was talking animatedly with Claes. Someone paid the check and we went noisily down the stairs and let ourselves be swallowed up by the carnival, which was in full swing in the narrow streets. People, some of them in costume, flowed from one end of town to the other in a tight throng, jumping, dancing, and wringing the last strength out of their tired bodies to the thudding of the drums and the shrill, seductive call of the bagpipes and the flutes. The trumpets screeched off-key. The clarinets wheezed and hoarse throats screamed. It was medieval. It was absurd.

But like everyone else I let myself be sucked in by the common pulse of the crowd. I had my arm around the clown girl's waist. I could feel the curve of her hips, and at times her breast pressed against my hand as we pushed and tumbled onward in the drunken masses. It stank of wine and garlic and sweat and makeup. The clown girl put her arm around my neck. We were almost the same height, and she laughed into my face. Every time the drunken throng forced us together, pushed us into a wall, our bodies would be glued together before we slipped out into the dance again. If we were about to lose each other she would grab hold of my hand or sling her arms around my neck, and now I had two spots of color on my cheeks from her makeup. The drums went on and on. The bagpipes played on and on. The flutes screeched higher and higher, and over everything boomed the fireworks. The crowd didn't want to stop. It continued its rhythmic swaying and pitching, a many-headed monster that filled the center of town and made all form of communication impossible except the purely physical. It was as if the knot in my soul loosened under the communal erotic release. For once I didn't fight it. If the person next to me jumped, I jumped higher. If the clown girl screamed along with the refrain in incomprehensible Basque words, I screamed even louder. I followed the others' dancing, swaying march forward, driven by desire and pain, with Claes' blond shock of hair like a beacon in front of me — through the dark night with my blood roaring in every cell. Dance! yelled every fiber, dance it out of you, disappear behind the protective cover of the mask, dance with them to the black gate of hell.

But that isn't where we ended up — it was a little plaza. Gasping and sweating, with inflamed eyes, we ordered cold draft beer that ran down our throats in long cool gulps. Then we looked at each other happily, hugged each other, and wished each other luck. Claes kissed the waitress, not noticing that when he bent to reach her mouth the beer poured out onto the cobblestones from the glass he was holding behind her back.

I was standing with my arm around the clown girl's waist, and she had her arm around me. Miguel stood there with his soda water, looking at us with a smile, but a little skeptically. And at that moment the feeling of liberation ended, the euphoria vanished, and I slipped back into my prison.

I removed my arm and fished out a cigarette. Offered one to

her too, but she shook her head and took out one of her own black ones. I lit it for her, and she carefully took my hand and held it in both of hers. The makeup on her cheeks cracked a little when she inhaled, and the glow of her cigarette shone in the dark.

She didn't move away; she kept standing close to me. She could almost look straight into my eyes. She was tall for a Spanish woman. I was short for a Danish man. Her eyes were gray and she smelled of theater makeup and garlic and black cigarettes and herself—and that spicy bouquet was one of the sexiest things I'd experienced in years. I was struck by a desire more powerful and desperate than I'd felt since I was with Charlotte for the first time, dancing with her one summer evening. Her body had been hot and sweaty too after many furious dances. Finally there was a slow dance and I could pull her to me and feel her body against mine in all its glory.

"What's your name?" I asked in Spanish in order to get out of my trance.

"They call me Ogoya," she said in English with almost no accent.

Ogoya? I could practically taste the name; I tried to scrutinize her face behind the thick theater makeup.

"You speak English?" I said instead.

"You sound like that's the strangest thing you've ever heard of."

"I haven't met very many Spaniards who can speak anything except Spanish."

"That's probably because I'm not a Spaniard."

"Are you English?"

"I'm Basque. *Una vasca*," she added in Spanish, but there was no anger in her voice. Claes came over to us. He was practically dragging the waitress with him. She was smiling happily up at him.

"Ogoya. *Hola. ¿Qué?*" said Claes.

"She speaks excellent English," I said stupidly.

"She speaks English like a native. She lived in England for a long time. But you should hear her Spanish — it's worse than yours."

"What did he say?" asked Ogoya.

"He said that your Spanish is worse than mine."

She let her arm slide around my waist and rested her clown head on my shoulder as she looked straight at Claes, even though she was talking to me.

"That could be true."

"That seems strange," I said.

"Why?"

"Because you live in Spain."

"In Euskadi. That's not the same thing." She pressed her hip against mine, slid around so she could clasp her hands behind my back and I could look into her eyes. Her eyes were shot through with fine red lines. Carnival fever. I tried to look behind the makeup to get a glimpse of her hidden face. Her lips tasted like makeup when she kissed me and her tongue tasted faintly of tobacco and beer as it quickly explored my mouth, slippery and cool.

I wanted to kiss her again, but she let go and stood there with her hip against mine. We had our arms around each other's waists.

Claes said in English, "Ogoya lived in the mountains with her father until she was sixteen. Would you believe it? Up in the mountains in a remote little valley, herding the sheep and goats. She didn't speak a word of Spanish until she was seventeen. You can find a lot of people like her here in the Basque country. It's incredible, isn't it? She couldn't read or write properly. Then the virgin of the valley was discovered by a nasty man from depraved San Sebastián — a man who brought her down from

the garden of Eden, took her virtue, taught her Spanish, sent
her to school, and initiated her into the decadence of the
world."

"Is that true?" I asked.

"It's almost true," she said.

"What part isn't?"

"The man who came and took me down from the mountain
wasn't nasty."

We all laughed. Miguel said something in Basque. Ogoya
answered. Whenever they spoke to each other they used that
strange language.

Ogoya took my hand.

"Come on!" she said. "Let's find another place to get a
drink."

"I have a meeting with the consul tomorrow."

She slowed her rapid pace.

"So? . . ."

"It's getting late."

"Your meeting with the consul isn't until tomorrow, is it?"

"That's right. That's what I said."

"Come on! Let's find another place where we can get a
drink. What happens tomorrow has nothing to do with you and
me right now."

I still held on to her hand, pulling her back.

"What happened to the man who wasn't nasty?" I asked.

She laughed.

"That's none of your business."

Then she started running, and I ran after her.

We came to a bar down by the harbor—the blue cutters lay
in the moonlight, and between the houses you could see out to
the island in the bay. The bar was right next to a huge building
built in the best wedding cake style. The bar was full of smoke
and young people, and above the music I could smell the spicy

hash, which reminded me of an almost forgotten youth, before my marriage and the kids had made their appearance.

Once again we let Claes act as the trailblazer. We followed his blond hair into the darkness of the room, rock music pounding in our ears. I felt great — drunk and sober at the same time, swaying and light on my feet. I hung on to Ogoya's hand; it was as if I were still dreaming, as if I had never woken up, as if I had experienced the past twenty-four hours through a piece of gauze. In the very back of the room there was a group of people sitting in low chairs of worn leather and rickety bamboo. They apparently knew Ogoya and Miguel and Claes, because after a general pushing and shoving and squeezing together, they made room for us.

Conversation was impossible, though people seemed to be ignoring that fact. Someone put a big glass of beer into my hand, and the whole thing reminded me of never-ending parties back home. They were enjoying themselves in the same desperate way as we do in Denmark when we have too much to drink and put on Dylan and Stones records to recapture our lost youth. I felt a little nauseated and tired. Ogoya's hand on my back was the only thing keeping me there. Her fingers crept slowly from the little hairs on the back of my neck all the way down to the belt under my jacket. I was so tired that I wasn't even surprised. The most exciting thing was probably that she was a faceless partner. The makeup covered her face. What did she look like? Her body was hidden by the folds of the clown costume. I only knew it as a softness felt in fleeting moments during the wild dance to the thudding rhythm of the carnival.

I felt like I was in a dream. I got a little idea of why charter trips are such a success: the possibility of unforeseen meetings under the influence of alcohol, the hope of the perfect love affair without illusion and without obligations.

The nausea increased, so I turned to Ogoya and mouthed

the word "toilet." She was engrossed in conversation in her
incomprehensible language with a man with a full beard and
little round glasses, who for some reason seemed familiar.
I think he was one of the four from the exile in Denmark.

She smiled, leaned forward, and kissed me again in the same
way — quick and hot. Her tongue just brushed my teeth and
then disappeared before I could return her kiss.

She pointed to a door on one of the walls. It was hard to see.
The light was dim. I was almost suffocating from the smoke,
which floated in solid streams toward the ceiling. All of the faces
flowed together and were difficult to separate.

The toilet was occupied, but there was no line outside.

I waited, swaying a little. The door opened and the man
from the embassy stepped out. I didn't recognize him at first.
I didn't connect the fringed leather jacket, the worn jeans, and
the dark sunglasses with the "Danish diplomat" from Madrid.
He had already become part of another world, part of something
that had happened a long time ago and that didn't concern me
anymore, something that had happened outside of my bell jar
and the remoteness I found myself in now.

But he recognized me immediately. And it was his recognition of me that triggered my memory of him. He reacted faster
and gave me a hard shove in the chest so I fell back against the
wall of humanity surrounding me. My semi-fall caused a chain
reaction and we fell like bowling pins struck by a particularly
lucky ball.

I got up through a tangled mass of arms and legs. The music
drowned out my shouts aimed at the fleeing yellow-leather back
shoving its way toward the door. I'm not a brave man. Physically, I've never been macho, either in the sports arena or when
things have gotten rough in a bar. But still, I pushed my way
toward the door and set out after the man from the embassy, the

Danish-speaking Lars Hansen, whom the switchboard operator at the hotel had called a Spaniard.

I kept pushing and shoving, ignoring protests and wrenching myself free from arms trying to hold me back and voices demanding an explanation, and finally I got out into the night.

Right or left? I chose left and ran a few steps until I reached an intersection. To the right the street led to the center of town. To the left there was the strong smell of the harbor and, from far away, muffled by the night, the sound of running feet. The noise of the carnival had faded. Only a few night wanderers and small groups were still drifting through the streets.

I took off running and reached the end of the row of houses. Up to the right I saw him running like a rat along the house wall. To the left lay the docks and the rocking fishing cutters and pleasure boats. The island was a black blob under the dark evening sky. He cut back into the town's grid of identical streets with their shuttered bars and the shops now protected by grates. Right or left? I chose right this time. Then another intersection and another choice. Right again. But he was gone.

My lungs wheezed and I forced myself to stand still and listen. And then I heard the shout. It was Claes.

"He's heading for the harbor again, Poul!"

I took off to the left and saw him running toward the pier, where fish restaurants lay in a row waiting for summer. Then he disappeared in the shadow of a jutting rock on one of the promontories that started to curve out into the bay there. In the flickering yellow light I caught sight of Claes and Miguel standing down by the other end, where I had first seen the man from the embassy. Again I forced myself to stand still and listen — the way I did during night hikes as a boy scout, when the darkness of the night would make my ears grow and absorb sounds, both close up and far away. I don't know where I got my courage

from or how I could ignore my pounding heart and the stabbing
fear in my throat.

"Stay where you are!" I yelled to Claes in Danish, without
thinking that the man from the embassy could understand
Danish, of course. "Cut him off!"

"What the hell happened? Who are you chasing?" yelled
Claes.

"It's the man from the embassy."

"Who? Who is it?" Claes shouted again, but I didn't answer
because the yellow leather jacket popped out of its hiding place
and ran effortlessly away on high-heeled boots whose taps click-
clacked against the cobblestones.

I broke into a run again, and sensed that Claes and Miguel
were running after me too. We ran along the dock. The pleasure
boats lay in rows, rocking in the light evening breeze, and you
could see straight across the bay and over to the promenade,
empty now at night, with the naked trees in the white light of
the round streetlamps. Then I lost sight of him again and just
about lost my balance when my foot caught on a projection on
the uneven dock surface. Where is he? I thought. Not: What are
you doing? He's bigger and stronger than you — you could tell
that when you were shoved hard in the chest and fell over. He
had the right jab of a boxer. You ought to be scared! Where is
that bastard, I thought, as if the years of suppressed rage at being
pushed around were infusing every fiber of my body. I wasn't
scared, didn't want to be scared anymore.

I stopped running and stood still. The boats lay there, sealed
and dark. I stood completely still; first I let my eyes search slowly
over the dock, then over the massive stone wall that shot up in
the dark with a stairway cut into it, and finally along the harbor
front itself, with its tall buildings. It was comforting to see the
few windows that were still lit. Miguel had vanished and Claes
was standing there lost, as if he didn't know whether he should

come over to me, stay where he was, or go toward the streets of the town. Hadn't he seen the yellow leather jacket disappear along the pier?

I heard the sound of the clicking heels. One, two, three. But I turned around too late. He gave me an almost apologetic look before I felt the push and fell sideways into the water and started to go to the bottom. The water was icy cold and tasted like oil. It got into my nose and throat and touched off a coughing reflex when I came up to the surface. Then I went under again, and it wasn't until the third time that the panic let go of me and I remembered my swimming lessons and the repeated advice: Stay calm. Don't panic.

I'm an excellent swimmer, in fact, and the third time I began to tread water while I tried to get my bearings. I was between two pleasure boats and had miraculously missed another set of mooring posts when I was pushed in. The water bit into my body, and my arms and legs felt heavy from the cold. With three strokes I swam over to the bulwark and reached up and got hold of Claes' outstretched hand. Supported by Miguel, he was leaning far down over the water. I saw Ogoya standing behind Miguel. Her clown face shone yellow as a corpse in the night. I got one hand up on a couple of timbers, my foot tried to find the slimy pilings under the water, and finally Claes got a solid grip on my hand. My mouth was swollen from the acrid taste of oil-polluted water.

Miguel came up and together they got me pulled onto land. I was shaking in the cold night, even after Miguel put his thick sheepskin coat around me. But we all started laughing with relief when my trembling fingers pulled a soggy cigarette out of my jacket pocket. My glasses had fallen off before I landed in the harbor. Ogoya stood with them in her hand and looked at me. Her face was veiled and dim before my nearsighted eyes, an even more mysterious funhouse mirror. Claes gave me a lighted cigarette. My fingers made two wet spots on it. We all smoked a cigarette before Claes asked, "What the hell happened?" He was speaking in Spanish.

"I saw the man from the embassy," I said in Danish. "He came out of the toilet. He knocked me down and took off. So I ran after him."

Claes looked at me dubiously.

"I'm absolutely positive."

"But why did you run after him?"

"Isn't that a pretty ridiculous question? Don't you think he owes us an explanation or two?"

"You're damn right. But people carry guns in this country. And it doesn't matter what side they're on. Goddamn it, Poul. I told you before — keep your nose out of things up here. They kill people at the drop of a hat."

His words sank in. I began to shake even harder, both from the cold and from fear. But I had to find out if anyone had recognized him. If anyone knew who he was.

"I only got a glimpse of his back," said Miguel in Spanish.

"I didn't see him at all, but I'll have Miguel look into it," said Ogoya in English, as if it were perfectly natural for Miguel to do things for her.

"Thanks," I said. "If nothing else, for Charlotte's sake."

She looked at me solemnly.

"From now on we do things for your sake, Poul."

She said something in Basque to Miguel, who nodded and disappeared at a run down the pier. I sat up with my back against a rough wall, shaking like mad. Claes and Ogoya pulled me up, one on each side, and we walked toward the lights of the town. Miguel arrived with a car and they put me in the back seat with Ogoya next to me. Claes crawled in front. We sat on a blanket and they put another dry blanket over my back and shoulders.

"What about your passport?" Claes asked me on the way to the hotel.

"Luckily it's still at the front desk with my traveler's checks and most of my money."

"I guess sometimes you're allowed to be lucky."

Sitting close to Ogoya, I agreed with him.

The woman at the front desk had been replaced by an older man who made sympathetic noises in Spanish and Basque when he saw me. But he didn't express any great surprise, as if it were a natural thing for a foreigner to fall into the harbor during carnival in San Sebastián.

They helped me up to my room. The bed was turned down, and the roar of the sea was faint through the closed shutters. Claes gave me a little smile, silent encouragement. More formal, Miguel came over to me and embraced me in a quick yet warm hug.

Ogoya stayed.

"Come on," she said, taking my hand and pulling me into the bathroom. I left a wet trail across the floor and my heart was pounding, but now it was for a different reason. In the bathroom she undressed me while the hot water ran in the tub and steam filled the room with heat and moisture. Slowly she removed my clothing, one piece at a time. First my jacket, then my sweater, then my shirt, which her fingers unbuttoned steadily without trembling.

She peeled the shirt off me. I was all blue from the cold. She loosened my belt and I stepped out of my pants and kicked them away. She knelt down and pulled off my wet socks while I sat on the edge of the bathtub. I was still shivering uncontrollably from the cold. I stood up and she let her hand slide all the way from the back of my neck down my back and in under the edge of my underpants and farther down as she pulled them off. Her hands were warm and soft, and the hot steam began to make me sweat.

"Come on," she said again, helping me into the tub. My whole body hurt as I sank into the hot water until I was completely covered, with my legs pulled up to my chin and room in the tub for one more.

She unzipped the clown costume in the back and stepped out of it. It was made of light fabric, so she had a black leotard on underneath. I looked at her without excitement as she pulled it off and lithely slipped out of her panties and let herself sink down into the water facing me.

The excitement came with the heat and with the first glimpse of her naked face, as she washed off the makeup and I gradually saw her emerge from behind the evening's mask.

9

The consul was well on his way to getting drunk, though it was only 10:30. He was a very short man. Only a little over 5'3", with receding gray hair and glasses that were much too big for his narrow, wrinkled face. It looked as if he used rouge, but it was only a criss-crossing of fine blood vessels on his face. He smelled of liquor and cologne, but he was impeccably dressed in a gray suit and white shirt with a little diamond stickpin in his blue striped tie. Was he 50 or 60 or older? With money he was fighting his body's decay, and he didn't waver as he got up from his place behind the desk and walked across the floor to take my outstretched hand in both of his as he gazed up at me.

I knew he was probably a bit loaded already, even though no one would ever see him really drunk. My own father had been like that until his liver had given out and he had slipped into such dissolution that even the finest clothes and the most expensive aftershave didn't help.

The consul's office was located a little way up the hill, and from the window you could see out over half the bay. Rain was moving in from the Bay of Biscay, but there was a thin line of light on the horizon that promised better weather. The office got a lot of light; with Finnish furniture and thin curtains it was so un-Spanish that the picture on the wall of the Danish royal couple in official attire didn't really fit in with the bright living-room decor.

The consul stood for a moment with my hand in his. He didn't say anything. I could still feel the warmth of the bed and the shower in my limbs and the memory of Ogoya's soft body in

every fiber. I felt cheerful, satisfied, and energetic despite only a
few hours of sleep. Finally he let go of my hand and, with an
elegant gesture, indicated that I should sit down in the chair
near the end table. I sank down into the chair and had to pull
myself up in order not to disappear in its depths. He sat on the
very edge of his chair; still without a word, he offered me a
cigarette from a little silver canister standing between two cups
and a very Danish-looking coffeepot.

He poured some coffee and said, "We are terribly sorry.
Please accept my family's and my deepest condolences. She was
a wonderful woman and a credit to freedom of speech."

I didn't say a word. He spoke Danish without an accent, but
with a slightly Jysk intonation. I don't know why, but I had
expected a Spaniard in this remote part of the Spanish kingdom,
not someone from Jylland dressed like the Rosenkavalier.

We both took a sip of coffee. I said, "I suppose there are
certain practical details regarding the transport of Charlotte's . . .
earthly remains?" It didn't sound right. Especially since I was
feeling so comfortable.

"Ah yes," said the consul, leaning forward. "Taking care of
practical matters can ease the sorrow. Your wife's death has
given us quite a lot to do, if one may say so. We're not com-
plaining, of course. Not at all. But the instructions from Madrid
were clear. We're to do whatever is within our modest power to
assist you. We understood that the instructions came from the
Foreign Ministry. The power of the press and all that. An important institution in modern society, it is said. More coffee?"

I hadn't eaten breakfast, so I said yes. I had to concentrate to
follow what he was saying. I was thinking the whole time about
Ogoya, who was still lying naked in bed with her round limbs
and warm breasts wrapped up in the blankets. That's how I had
left her, with a kiss on her lips after a night that had rejuvenated
me following months of celibacy.

"And perhaps we should enjoy a small brandy with our morning coffee, considering the rawness of the day."

It was more a statement than a question. The rawness of the day must mean the rain that was beating against the window; I could see it drifting in long sheets across the bay, almost obscuring the island in the middle. The beach was dark yellow and abandoned. The sea was gray with long heavy swells. But there was no rawness inside of me — a bright sunshine was still shining even though incipient melancholy was about to set in.

He poured a couple of large brandies into the glasses that were already standing there. His hand shook a little after all.

"Are you a religious man, Mr. Jensen?" he asked with his glass raised.

Should I answer or take a drink? I drank.

"No, I don't think so. I was baptized, and I guess I'm a member of the state church too, but it's been years since I set foot in a church."

"Ah yes, we Danes — one remembers the superficiality. We asked because we imagine that religion can help one through the difficult battles of the soul, strengthen one in the struggle with grief, as it were, so that one comes out of the battle healed. Like a broken leg which is stronger where it grew back together than anywhere else."

He took another sip and looked at me expectantly.

"I don't think I follow you."

"We're not expressing ourselves clearly. We hope that we expressed ourselves more clearly to your colleagues who called yesterday and today."

"What colleagues?"

"Representatives of the press. These ladies and gentlemen seem to take a morbid interest in the life of your deceased wife." He clucked his tongue, as if he found the very expression distasteful.

"I'm not a journalist," I said.

He raised his eyebrows, with his mouth pursed over the glass. His large spectacles had a tendency to slip down his nose.

"You're not?" he said. "We had the impression you were."

"I'm a jurist."

"Congratulations. An honorable profession. With all due respect for the soul of your wife, the occupation of a journalist reminds me a great deal of the work of a prostitute — indispensable in modern society for providing man with pleasure and satisfaction, but at the cost of love and money. The price may fluctuate, but in the long run there is a price. A jurist, indeed."

I was beginning to get sick and tired of the consul's babblings and reactionary outpourings. I didn't even find him interesting. I don't like stupid people, and I'm not fascinated by idiocy. Charlotte could spend hours talking to totally boring people just because she believed that everybody, somewhere inside, had a story to tell.

"There were certain practical matters?" I tried again.

"Ah yes. The instructions were clear. We are to assist you. Do you speak Spanish, Mr. Jensen?"

"A little."

"Excellent. We have a name to give you. A business card and an address, right near the old Casino, the City Hall. There is a police commissioner in charge of the case; he has all the papers. We have spent considerable time on the case, and everything should be in order, we believe."

"A police commissioner?"

"Yes. That's what they said. They wish to ask you a few questions. Purely routine, they assured us. After that you sign a couple of papers and then your wife will be delivered to you."

I couldn't hold back a giggle that sounded like a schoolgirl's.

"We fail to see the humor."

"Excuse me. I haven't been myself the last few days."

"We understand. Have another pick-me-up. We aren't Swedes, after all."

Was he trying to be funny?

"I only mean, what am I supposed to do with my deceased wife after they deliver her to me?"

"Ah . . . we see the problem. That's all taken care of. As we said, the instructions were clear. The case will be covered in detail by the press, of course, so we have done everything to assist you. We have taken the liberty of arranging the rental of a vehicle which can transport Mr. Jensen and his wife's body to Madrid and there make connections with an SAS flight to Copenhagen."

He seemed nervous. I left my glass untouched, but he took a drink from his now and then. Small, dainty sips. Only his language was exaggerated. Everything else about him was refined and discreet, but he was also nervous and high-strung.

"You mean a hearse, that I have to drive to Madrid myself?"

He looked at me, horrified.

"Isn't that satisfactory?"

"Oh, definitely. I am very grateful for your assistance."

"We try our best."

We sat there a while, listening to the rain, which made me keep forgetting that I was in Spain. I was sitting in a Danish living room, speaking Danish, and listening to the rain. It was unreal. The very topic of conversation was unreal.

"These are not easy matters to talk about," I said. My tongue was beginning to loosen because of the brandy on an empty stomach. I was starving, and I started to mix up food fantasies with erotic images.

"Oh yes. We realize that. That's why we asked if you were religious. We actually meant Catholic. A rather stupid question,

we admit. But when one has lived here for years and is married
to a Basque woman of the Catholic faith, one easily takes things
for granted."

I looked at him, bewildered.

He went on. "Down here they have a different relationship
to death. Back home we cultivate respect for the body of the
deceased. We honor it and talk about it in whispers. The Spanish word for corpse is 'cadaver.' To Danish ears it seems a word
which precisely describes the Spaniard's attitude to the flesh.
Here the mass for the soul is more important than the burial
itself. The earthly remains are merely the vessel of the soul and
can hardly demand the same kind of respect, don't you agree?"

"Why are you telling me all this?"

He looked at me, a little hurt. Straightened the impeccable
knot of his tie with slim fingers. Lit another long filter cigarette.

"Are we boring you?"

"That's not what I said. I asked why you're telling me all
this."

"To make an attempt to explain that you may later experience a certain, shall we say, contempt for your wife's earthly
remains — contempt which you will perceive as contempt for
something you hold sacred, but which we beg you to understand
has nothing to do with respect for Mrs. Damsborg. Honor the
soul — to hell with the body, so to speak." Once again that dry
laugh, as if to explain away his stylistic lapse. I was still just as
confused.

"I know she's dead," I said, annoyed. "I have voluntarily
agreed to take her home so she can be buried. That means a lot
to her mother too. Goddamn it, Spain is a civilized country,
isn't it? It must be possible to arrange things practically so all this
can be done under the proper hygienic conditions."

"Naturally. Everything has been arranged according to the
instructions."

"Thank you."

Again we sat listening to the rain. There wasn't really any-thing else to say, but I was somehow unable to get up. His gloominess held me, increasing my own melancholy, which was nourished by the liquor from the day before and the mem-ory of Ogoya's body in the dim light, with the sound of the slowly crashing waves mingling with the pounding of our blood.

He leaned back in his chair, almost vanishing in its great embrace. He flicked his cigarette and delicately put it out. His face was now a shade redder, as if you could count the emptied bottles in every broken blood vessel.

"Have you lived here a long time?" I asked.

"Oh yes. More than thirty years. We sold wine to Scandi-navia before the Irma supermarkets made Spanish wine a house-hold word. We have had our business deals, made money, and minded our own affairs. Kept out of trouble, but still . . ."

"Still what?"

"Do you have any children, Mr. Jensen?"

"Two small children."

"They're nice when they're little. One hasn't had the plea-sure of having grandchildren yet."

"You have children yourself?"

"Yes, a grown son."

"Does he live here?"

The consul got up on rather unsteady legs, tugged at his jacket in the back, went over to the window and stared out across the bay. He stood with his hands behind him, rocking back and forth on his feet like an old schoolteacher who is bored with life's eternal repetitions. There are no new children under the sun.

"He's studying in France," he said without turning around. Looking out at the rain, he continued, "I was an anti-fascist during the war. Did my small part. I want you to know that first."

His tone had changed character . . . and wasn't that the first time he had used the first person?

"One did one's part," he continued, as if talking to himself. "One didn't want to be lumped together with Franco, may his soul forever rot in the fires of hell. But there has to be a limit. Especially today, when there are completely different rules to the game. It has to be stopped. The murders, the taxes, the graft in the Commissariat. A solution must be found so everybody can come home and we can all live in peace with each other."

He turned around. His eyes were wet.

"It must quite simply cease," he said emphatically. Then he seemed to pull himself together. As if he couldn't decide whether to explain himself further or send me out into the rain with a bit of practical advice. He acted rather like me. You can keep the lid on a lot of boiling emotions by replacing them with concrete, mundane activities.

"Ah well," he said. "Ah well. Someday it will just have to stop." Now his voice was subdued. He had decided, but I never found out what the decision entailed, because at that moment a large woman his age came into the office. She said something to him in Basque. He nodded. She repeated her words. He nodded harder. Then she smiled at me coldly and left. It was as if she had never been there, but her presence lingered in the room.

"My wife," he said. "With a reminder not to forget an important meeting."

He seemed like the kind of man whose all too empty calendar seldom included important meetings. But I didn't care. I would have liked to question him some more, but Ogoya's body pulled at me more strongly and won out over my curiosity.

He rummaged in his desk. The top of it was painfully neat. He found a business card, which he gave me along with his own.

"Your appointment is at 5:30. At the Commissariat. Can you make it?"

"Of course."

He took me lightly by the arm and led me out into the hall. He held on to my arm just above the elbow.

"Conveniently enough there's a taxi stand right at the bottom of the stairs. Again — we're deeply sorry, but allow us to thank you for a pleasant morning."

"Don't mention it. I'm the one who should thank you." I was getting caught up in his rituals and I wanted to leave, but he kept on holding my arm.

"We would hope that you would keep in mind what we tried our best to tell you."

I didn't know what he was talking about. My brain was functioning slowly and I wanted to get away from there as fast as possible.

"Mr. Jensen. You must understand. One doesn't always make one's own choices. Sometimes choices are made in someone else's behalf. One tries to do one's duty. It's not always easy."

"You've done what you could. It's not your fault that my wife is dead." He let go of me and stepped back. "You're not responsible for all the political violence that goes on in the world."

"That's not what we were insinuating."

"Neither was I."

"One just hopes that you will bear in mind what was said to you. That's all."

His wife was standing like a shadow at the end of the hall, looking down at us. She didn't say anything, but his glance darted back at her. The consul gave me a brief, limp handshake and held open the door so I could leave. It wasn't raining anymore, but the heavy clouds looked as though they might open up again at any moment. The weather was apparently just as changeable as in Denmark.

Suddenly something became blindingly clear to me.

"I think I met your son yesterday," I said to the half-open door. The door stopped moving, and he stuck out his head again. His face had turned white.

"That's impossible," he said.

I shrugged my shoulders. "Thanks for a pleasant morning," I said.

I started to leave. He looked as if he wanted to come after me. But he gave up the idea midway and slammed the door shut.

I stood waiting for a taxi. The clouds were lifting. The heavy rain was drifting out over the sea and behind the mountains surrounding the town.

I heard footsteps behind me, and when I turned around I saw the heavy-set, black-haired woman from the consul's apartment. She had pulled a shawl over her head. She came right up close to me. Her flat brown shoes slapped the pavement. She had on a black skirt and a dark blue sweater. A pretty brooch fastened the shawl across her breast. She was a big woman without being fat, and she wasn't wearing any makeup. Her face was angular, and I got the impression that behind all the sternness she had once been beautiful. She still had enough pride to carry her head very high.

"Excuse me, *señor*," she said in clear Spanish.

I didn't answer, just smiled.

"I don't know what kind of lies that old fool of a drunken husband of mine has been telling you, but don't believe a word he said." Her voice was hard as metal. Like a rasping file.

"I don't know what you're talking about."

"It's all lies."

"We were talking about my wife."

She was silent for a moment.

"And about my son?"

"No, not about him."

"Then you must excuse me, *señor*." She turned around, but changed her mind and then said, "You see, *señor*, my husband is not just a drunk. He's a liar too. He lies to himself. He's a dreamer. He dreams about a son lost long ago."

"Lost?"

"Our son died many years ago, *señor*. *Adiós, señor*."

I shouted after her, "How did he die?"

"The Communists killed him," she said. "Whatever they may say, the Communists killed him."

She vanished just as quickly as she had appeared.

Then a taxi finally showed up. I gave everything a lot of thought during the cab ride back. Spent ten minutes on the first bit of analytical work I had done in days. And various pieces began to fall into place. At least I thought so at the time, though I was still left with a lot of unanswered questions.

The front desk clerk received me coldly. She blocked my way to the elevator and asked me to step into the sitting room.

"You're only paying for a single room," she said.

I nodded.

"You will be charged the price of a double room tonight."

"OK."

"Will you also be needing a double room for the next few nights?"

"I don't know."

She looked even angrier. "Do you think this is proper?"

"I thought Claes Hylander had stayed here."

I had her there, but she made a quick comeback. "Señor Hylander isn't married."

"Neither am I." I took the stairs instead of the elevator. Young Mr. Jensen is sure changing, I thought, exhilarated.

Ogoya was talking on the phone when I came into the room. She had opened the shutters slightly, and the first rays of sunshine were sneaking in. She was lying on her stomach, naked, speaking Basque, as she lazily kicked her legs in the air. The remains of breakfast were on a tray on the floor. I took off my clothes. She turned over on her back and put down the phone just as I got out of my underpants and kicked them into a corner. She was enjoying her own body; she stretched and reached out her arms to me.

"Come here," she said, just like the night before.

Afterwards we lay there for a long time, silent, smoking cigarettes. I was lying on my back. She was on her side, resting on her elbow as she drew letters on my naked chest.

"I talked to Miguel," she said at last. "He found out who knocked you in the water yesterday."

"I think I know who it was."

Her fingers stopped and then started drawing again.

"Who?"

"I don't know his name, but I've just been with his father."

The expression on her face confirmed it.

"The consul's son," I said.

"You're very clever," she said, blowing smoke down into my face.

"I'm also very hungry."

She stubbed out her cigarette, then took mine and put it out too. She slid down my chest, over my stomach, and down between my legs. I felt her soft lips and her tongue all the way down.

"There's plenty of time," she said. "We don't have to meet Miguel for an hour."

"What did he find out?"

"Be quiet. There's plenty of time."

I shut up.

10

She was different from Charlotte. Not just in appearance, but also in temperament. Charlotte had been blonde, slim, intelligent, efficient, and well-dressed without being snobbish about it. Ogoya was rounder and softer. Beneath her dark hair she had an open, almost childlike face, as if life hadn't touched her, even though she must have been close to thirty, or possibly older. Ogoya was not as verbal as Charlotte either. Whatever it was she was thinking about, she kept it to herself. It wasn't a language problem. Her English was practically flawless. Better than mine, in fact.

We walked along the promenade in the sun, which had popped out like a genie from a bottle and turned San Sebastián into a chalk-white town surrounded by a postcard-blue sea that disappeared from sight out beyond the bay.

We walked holding hands, no longer alone, because the sunshine had brought people out in droves. The tide was on its way out and we could see down to the beach from the promenade. Little boys had drawn soccer fields in the damp sand and put up goal nets. They had already started playing, and you could see it was deadly serious — they had club uniforms and real soccer shoes, and their shouts rang through the air. The perennial joggers were running along the edge of the water, and there were plenty of dogs too.

We walked briskly, hand in hand, in the sunshine.

"It's lucky it's good weather," said Ogoya, smiling.

"Your climate is like ours," I said.

"Only warmer," she said. It was February, but the air felt like a nice May day in Denmark.

Suddenly I noticed a torn poster, hanging limply from a lamppost. It was for a long-forgotten evening of poetry and music, and half of Ogoya's sultry face stared down at the passersby. I stopped and held her back with my hand.

"Look, it's you," I said. "What does it say?"

"It says that I read poems and sing Basque songs."

She let go of my hand and ran off toward Claes' hotel. She was a refreshing sight in her clown suit amid the crowds. People had on their good clothes today. It must be a holiday. The children all looked perfectly washed and combed. I felt wonderful. I was seventeen again. I ran after her, grabbed her hand, swung her around, pulled her to me and kissed her. I got her "public" kiss again, the bird peck with the quick tongue that gently touched mine.

"I didn't know you could write poetry and sing."

"There's a lot you don't know about me."

We had reached the hotel where Claes was staying. A great white colossus that lay like a ship in front of the plaza by the city hall. Ogoya stopped.

"I have to go home now," she said.

"Will we see each other soon?"

"I just have to change my clothes. Tonight all of San Sebastián will dress in black."

"In black? What for?"

"Because tonight we will bury the Sardine."

I looked at her in surprise, holding her around the waist.

"You'll see," she said.

I held her tight.

"When will I see you again?"

"Miguel told me to tell you that he has some information for you. He's up in Claes' room. Go on up to him now, my love."

"So when do I meet you again?"

"Later." Again the fleeting kiss, then she pulled herself free. As she left I said, "What did Miguel find out?"

"Ask Miguel."

Then I called after her, "What do you do when you're not writing poetry or singing songs?"

She turned around and blew me a kiss.

"Make love," she shouted back, and the clown suit disappeared in the crowd on the plaza. I went through the hotel's swinging door, singing idiotically: "Only sixteen, I'm only sixteen . . ."

"Oh great, that's a cute idea," said Claes. He was standing just inside the door with tired red eyes in a tense face. Miguel was standing a little behind him, as usual, smiling.

"*Hola*," he said. "I have something to tell you."

"I'm hungry," I said, not paying any attention to Claes. There was no sign of his waitress.

"Don't be so grouchy," said Claes. "I've just saved you from a fate worse than death."

"Which is?"

"Danish tabloid reporters. They called me up. I sent them to Vitoria. Said you were on your way to claim the body in the Basque capital. That you were practically dead with grief." He laughed.

"Thanks."

"I didn't say a word about you being here, fucking your brains out with Basque ladies."

"That was nice of you," I said with what coolness I could muster, but it still gave me a guilty conscience. Not because of poor Charlotte, but because I hadn't called home to ask about my kids. How were they right now? Jakob was in kindergarten, Stine was at the day care. Did they miss me? It seemed like I never had time to sit still for a single minute. I was on a disk that

was spinning faster and faster, and its centrifugal force was dragging me along, forcing me out to the edge. I was constantly
being led by the hand, from one event to the next, without
having time to absorb it all in my semi-conscious, alcohol-
ridden, sleepless condition.

"Let's find a cafeteria," said Miguel. "Come on."

We left. On the way I asked Claes why he stuck around at
all, why he helped out. He stopped in mid-stride and breathed a
wave of liquor into my face.

"I'll tell you why, my friend. First of all, I liked Charlotte.
And so I want to help you. Second, I've started to like *you*. And
want to help you. Third, I smell a story that might go and make
Mr. Hylander famous and earn him a pile of money in the
foreign press. And finally, Mr. Hylander needs a lot of money
for his personal use, I'll tell you that."

"And which reason is most important?"

"That doesn't matter."

"So it wasn't just for friendship's sake that you sent the
Danish reporters on a wild goose chase?"

"It was both. You scratch my back . . ."

"And I'll scratch yours."

"Goddamn right. I can tell you were married to Charlotte."

Miguel had been waiting patiently for us to finish. The
cafeteria was called The California. We ordered a little to eat
and something to drink, and then Miguel said, "We call him
Paxti. I thought he was dead. He's been missing for a year. He
was once my best friend. It's a very long story."

I heard part of the story there and part of it over lunch at the
same restaurant where we had eaten the night before. Miguel
told most of it; Claes helped with the language, and later Ogoya
joined us and she told me the rest.

Miguel and Paxti had met each other as thirteen-year-olds.
Miguel had come down from the mountains a year before. It

was the local priest in the isolated valley who had noticed the intelligence, the thirst for knowledge, the desire to learn hidden behind that sullen, handsome exterior. The priest wanted to help him and sent him to the Jesuit school near San Sebastián. Miguel's parents let him go only very reluctantly. They needed his labor on the little farm, but the padre's word carried a lot of weight. The voice of the church had guided the family's lives for generations.

The first year was hell for the boy. Miguel could only express himself in broken Spanish. Basque was his mother tongue, but the Jesuits whipped the Castilian language into him. And the official beatings were followed up with just as many unofficial ones in the schoolyard. Miguel was strong, sinewy, and tough from the many years in the mountains, but the Spanish-speaking boys were in the majority and let the shepherd's son know that they were the bosses here.

But he stuck it out. He immersed himself in studying. His time would come.

And then one day Paxti arrived. Pedro Peter Martínez y Irujo Jensen. A curiosity. A mixture. A blond madman with blue eyes and the strength of a Viking in the body of a little boy. A Danish father, who had made a lot of money in wine, shipping, steel, and chemicals down in Bilbao's reeking industrial hell. And a Basque mother. More Spanish than Danish, but he still spoke both languages. He had learned Danish partly at home from his father, partly during the long summer vacations in Denmark. Spanish was his native tongue. His mother was Basque, all right, but from the aristocracy. Her heart was in Madrid, as they said in San Sebastián.

And yet it was Paxti who brought the idea of revolution into Miguel's life. As so often before it was the children of the upper class who decided to lead the sons of the proletariat. It was in the mid-sixties, and the news of the Vietnam war was mixed with the echoes of the war for liberation which had been fought in Algeria. Paris 1968 was approaching, and the new youth movement in the U.S. and Europe sent waves all the way to San Sebastián, which was otherwise held in the firm grip of the dictatorship, like the rest of Spain.

There was already an organization in place. The ETA. It stood for "Basque Country and Freedom." Founded under the inspiration of Algeria's struggle for freedom from the French colonial powers. Wasn't the Basque territory colonized by Spanish conquerors in the same way? Was the oppression any different? Shouldn't they fight against it? Fight with guns in their hands. Had any people ever won their freedom with a rosary?

Paxti led the discussions after he and Miguel became friends. Paxti was a handsome fellow. Charming and aggressive, with the natural self-confidence of a rich man's son. Perhaps Paxti saw the potential in the sullen shepherd boy. He glimpsed the qualities that set Miguel above the other boys: all they ever talked about on their way home from school was soccer heroes and girls' crotches and budding breasts, which jiggled beneath their dresses in spite of the obligatory breast armor.

When Miguel became Paxti's friend, the persecution and teasing stopped. As his command of the Spanish language grew, he won the respect of his classmates and the padres, who may have been brutal but who also respected intelligence and the quest for knowledge.

In the beginning Paxti protected Miguel. He gave him strength and self-confidence and received loyalty and friendship in return. So when Paxti finally found a cause, it was obvious that Miguel would follow and devote his heart and soul to it, as well as his analytical powers, which had already earned him top marks in math and related subjects.

The cause was the historical right to self-determination of the Basque country, Euskadi; Paxti joined the struggle after a long summer vacation in Denmark. There he had come in contact with the Latin American and Spanish exile community, which was seething with revolutionary fervor. Back in Spain the Franco dictatorship had clamped a lid on all literature and others sources of revolutionary inspiration, but in Denmark you could get materials in English, Danish, and Spanish.

And then there were the first contacts with the ETA. Revolution was just around the corner. The Franco dictatorship would soon fall. The sick capitalist system and the bankrupt geriatric communism of the Soviet Union would also collapse soon, like the flimsy house of cards they were. I remember those days myself, and I can vividly picture Paxti returning to San Sebastián with the right contacts and full of new ideas.

Miguel had been helping his father in the mountains the whole summer, and he was looking forward to seeing Paxti, who arrived in San Sebastián with his bag full of illegal pamphlets and his heart overflowing with revolutionary zeal. They were only sixteen years old.

It wasn't difficult to convince Miguel. During his childhood his deeply religious father and mother had impressed on him the virtues of a conservative Christianity, but from the time he was very small he had also been imprinted with the idea that all the evil in the world came from Madrid.

So that autumn they would often sit in Paxti's well-furnished room, listening to the latest rock music and discussing revolution, Marxism, and the ETA, whose actions were still few and far between. That year the ETA killed its first Spanish officer, a notorious torturer. Otherwise there were just a few Basque flags hung up here and there, some slogans painted on the walls, and small, ineffectual bombs.

Franco was secure in his power. In Paxti's house they were free to be revolutionary, protected by his businessman father's respectability and his honorary consul title from the Danish government.

But preparing for revolution wasn't the only thing they did

together. That autumn they also lost their virginity with the same woman, paid for with the consul's money. They did their homework together, and they began to have girlfriends their own age. They were inseparable.

As often happens, the teacher–student roles became reversed. Miguel was by far the more gifted of the two. Paxti was superficial — fast cars, a quick screw on the back seat, bar-hopping downtown, "full steam ahead and don't look back." Miguel thought deeply about things. Whenever he reached a conclusion, he would act on it without wavering. Not that he denied himself pleasure. Far from it. Revolution meant liberation: sexual, economic, national, and personal.

Later on Miguel had mixed feelings about this period. On the one hand it meant the development of his political consciousness and the personal liberation of this reticent, inhibited shepherd's son. On the other hand it put him in a position of dependence on Paxti, so that his own self almost merged with Paxti's.

But more than anything else, Miguel began to understand. He concluded that the childhood poverty, the persecution, the beatings, the feeling of inferiority were all a result of a governmental oppression originating in Madrid. His gratitude to Paxti for leading the way was overwhelming. Paxti was the one who had lifted him up. Paxti was the one who had opened his eyes.

So when they were contacted by the organization, they were more than ready. Paxti because it appealed to his hunger for adventure. Miguel because it seemed the logical next step in a political process. The fascist dictatorship must of course be fought with guns in hand. Down through history, hadn't those in power always referred to freedom fighters as terrorists?

There was nothing romantic about it. They learned to know fear, uncertainty, and powerlessness. They saw their friends and lovers arrested and tortured by Franco's *guardia civil* and the police. They found out how poorly armed and badly organized the people's army was, and they discovered how much time was wasted on internal ideological squabbles that led to factionalism and impotence. But they also discovered that among the Basque people they were respected and supported, and in the foreign press they were called true freedom fighters struggling against a rock-hard dictatorship. In the Spanish press they were just bloodthirsty terrorists.

By 1970 the majority of the ETA leadership was in prison. At a military tribunal in Burgos, sentences of death or long prison terms were handed down to leaders who had not yet turned thirty. It was a young organization. Now there was room for Paxti and Miguel at the top. Miguel had developed into one of the most important theoreticians in the movement and was the mastermind behind a number of successful operations. Miguel was the brains. Paxti was the muscle.

Miguel was a clever tactician, who in Paxti had a faithful warrior. The roles had been reversed, and the blood on their hands was a personal bond that also tied them to the life they had chosen. There was no turning back.

Paxti had come to terms with his intellectual limitations and threw his strength, his coldbloodedness, and his steely nerve even more vigorously into the struggle that was filling the prisons with their friends and comrades.

They planned attacks. Their striking power increased. The life as semi-outlaws, the secret runs across the French border, the guns, the explosives, the respect, and the feeling of power got into their blood. After the empty years of his youth, Paxti in particular found meaning in the spine-tingling excitement and fear during the operations. And deep inside himself he found meaning in the killing, with its mixture of sweetness and pain.

The high point of their work together came in 1973, when Franco's heir, Admiral Blanco, and his car were blown sixty feet

in the air in a side street next to the headquarters of the Security
Police at Puerta del Sol in Madrid. The explosives in a tunnel
under the car had done their work. The culmination of Paxti
and Miguel's apprenticeship was an unqualified success.

The subsequent oppression from the system was tremendous. Its rage knew no bounds. Mass arrests and a declaration of
martial law followed.

The consul's protection worked again — for his son. The
consul got a tip from a police connection. That Paxti was under
suspicion as well. That he had better take off for France. The
consul expressed his gratitude with many green 1,000-peseta
bills in an envelope, while he feverishly started searching for his
only child. He had long since lost contact with him, and he
would have rejected him if the woman he had married hadn't
insisted that he was their own flesh and blood—the fruit
of a passion which had now been replaced by contempt and
indifference.

The consul had money. And the money found Paxti, but
Paxti never found Miguel. Why not? Nobody knows. Did he try
to trace his comrade-in-arms, or did he just look out for his own
skin? At any rate, they say he heard about Miguel's arrest on the
evening Spanish broadcast by Radio France from Saint-Jean-
de-Luz in the south, in the French Basque province. No one
had warned Miguel.

Now his days in hell would begin.

They started in with ordinary beatings. They used bare fists,
they used nightsticks, and they used rubber hoses. Then they
moved on to *falange*: they stripped him and laid him on his back
on a table, then they beat the soles of his feet to bloody ribbons.
Then they gave him the Bathtub: they forced his head over and
over again into a tub of filthy, stinking water filled with excrement, vomit, hair, and urine. His own vomit mixed with the

others'. Then they threw him into a cell and left him, shivering, alone with his tears. He hadn't said a word.

There were three of them, and they came back in the morning, when they woke him up and let him try the bathtub again before they got him into his clothes and tossed him in the back of one of their Land Rovers. They had pulled a hood down over his head, and he blindly felt the unevenness of the road with every bump, which made the pain shoot through his body. He knew that he was going to die. He could tell that they were heading up into the mountains. On the way up they beat him again. They concentrated especially on his kidneys and genitals this time. For the sake of appearances they asked some questions, but seemed uninterested in the answers. They didn't want answers. Their assignment was humiliation.

He could smell the clear air and the scent of pine trees when, swearing and cursing him, they shoved him out of the Land Rover. He felt the pistols in the back of his neck and his spine, and prepared himself to die. He doesn't remember much of what he was thinking. He cannot or will not recall the sensations or feelings that gripped him. He tensed his body, and time stood still, until he heard the shots ring in the air and then the drunken laughter of the *guardia civil*. They heaved him, shaking with fear and cold, back into the Land Rover after the faked execution. He fell into a restless sleep as they drove and drove, and didn't really wake up until he could hear what seemed like the noise of a big city through the cloth of the hood.

It was Madrid. Puerta del Sol. The headquarters of the Security Police.

They threw him into a new cell, where he lay he doesn't know how long, until they came to get him again, punching and kicking him down a long corridor. He still had the hood over his head, but he could feel that he was in a cellar where the air was sterile and cold, like a hospital. They stripped him again and laid him on a table and tied down his wrists and ankles so he lay stretched out on his back. His body ached and he was very hungry and thirsty.

They pulled off the hood, and he stared up at a thin, friendly face with a mustache. "Hello," said the delicate lips. "Welcome to Madrid. Now you are no longer protected by your dear Basque fatherland. Now you are in Madrid. And here we do what we want with you. Now we want some answers."

The first pain came when the man with the mustache ground out his cigarette on Miguel's naked chest. But strangely enough that was the only brutal act the man with the mustache performed himself. To Miguel it seemed as though he only wanted to show the other butchers that he was still capable of inflicting pain, although in reality he was past that stage in his career. As if the whole point of his life was to get the thick dossiers of information they had on Miguel to agree, to match, to add up.

That was only the beginning; he had helpers to do the dirty work. The man with the mustache maintained a cool politeness. He never raised his voice, always addressed Miguel as "Usted," and appeared spotless and pure in that inferno of blood and vomit, terror and screams, which Miguel endured for what seemed to him an eternity, but which in reality lasted barely three days.

They hung him up on the Parrot Perch with his wrists tied to his ankles and an iron rod inserted so that the weight of his whole body hung from his wrists. And then they beat him with clubs while he hung there like a helpless bird.

But the most horrible thing was the electrodes on his earlobes, tongue, rectum, and genitals. The electricity was applied in a scientific and cold-blooded manner, with a physician present who made sure that he survived. It was the scientific aura about it that did him in, Miguel explained. He could resist and tense his body in the anticipation of blows and punches dealt by men with distorted, hate-filled, raging faces. But he had no defense against the variable, shifting pain of the electric current, guided by a calm, passionless hand. In the course of those three days, like others before him, he told everything he knew to the friendly man with the mustache, who at the end thanked him for a pleasant conversation in a tone that held no trace of irony.

They didn't throw him back in a cell, but took care of him and nursed him, patched him up and healed the physical wounds and prevented him from dying. They had broken him, so they could afford to be indulgent. Furthermore, not even Franco's judges wanted any visible traces of the art of persuasion on the defendants when they were brought forward with their papers duly signed.

Then came the lengthy pretrial imprisonment, the trial, and the sentencing.

Miguel, along with a number of others, was sentenced to death.

Paxti was stuck in France, indirectly sentenced to live as an outlaw because his name was irretrievably linked to the organization. He couldn't come back. Like others, he had to wait until Franco died.

In September 1975 the Franco regime executed five young political resistors, despite vehement international protests. It was said that the executions made Paxti explode with rage. An impotent anger seized him. He swore revenge, and he spent nights planning possible escape attempts. But all in vain. He had been put on a sidetrack, and when Franco finally drew his last breath Paxti was in Paris. Officially, he was studying, but in reality he had turned into an alcoholic professional revolutionary on the left bank of the Seine, kept alive by the consul's money. No one knows for sure what his inmost thoughts were at that time, but everyone says that he looked and acted like a person who was plagued by a profound sense of guilt.

With Franco's death Miguel knew that his death sentence would never be carried out. Nevertheless, he masterminded a daring escape attempt a year later. Along with most of the others he was captured again, of course, but both the guards and the prisoners knew that an epoch had come to an end.

Democracy was on its way. With it came the political amnesty and the chance to start a new life.

In prison Miguel had continued his studies. He still had a passion for the Basque cause, but he knew that in a parliamentary democracy, armed actions would not be regarded as a struggle for freedom, but as terrorism — both in Spain and abroad. He no longer believed that guns were the answer.

Paxti returned from exile and immediately started talking to Miguel about new armed operations. What began as political discussions ended in fuming arguments between the old friends. Words flew through the air, getting more and more poisonous — traitor, coward, running off to France on your father's money, where were you while the rest of us were doing time.

It ended with animosity and a breakup. Paxti appointed himself the leader of what he called the Autonomous Commandos, and together with a new generation of young men in the military ETA he started in on a campaign of terror that left more dead after one year than during the entire Franco dictatorship.

The torture went on. The oppression went on. The killings went on.

But the friendship was over. They went their separate ways, and their paths seldom crossed. Miguel became a journalist and writer, Paxti a wanted terrorist, driven into a life that somehow seemed to him to be the only kind of existence that would give him excitement, meaning, satisfaction, and escape. As he once

confessed to Miguel, he had to escape from the emptiness that
had haunted him since puberty, when he played Russian rou-
lette with his father's revolver for the first time. At that instant he
understood that standing face to face with death makes you
value life afterwards. That it's only possible to endure life at the
moment you decide to die.

When in reality it's merely a question of choosing the right
moment.

11

Ogoya put out her cigarette. "It's strange," she said, "but the break with Paxti was hardest for Miguel. Because it was so total. He saw their disagreements as ideological and political. He thought Paxti was ignorant because he didn't understand. But Miguel didn't take it personally, at least not at first."

I looked at her curiously unlined face. Miguel and Claes had left, and Ogoya had finished the story over coffee. I had avoided looking at Miguel while Claes told me about the torture. It was as if he were intruding on Miguel's privacy, offending his sense of modesty. I don't care to talk about myself in public either, and I'm embarrassed by other people's all too obvious soul-searching in front of an audience. But Miguel had sat there with a stone face and hadn't acted like he was embarrassed. I couldn't understand how you could go on living after an experience like that. But cars still drove along the streets, buildings were still torn down or put up again, and you ate, drank, and made love as if nothing had happened.

Ogoya apparently knew the whole story, so I asked her, "Where do you fit into the picture?"

She looked up and took her time lighting another cigarette.

"I'm married to Miguel. He is my husband."

She must have had a malicious streak in her, because she enjoyed my stunned reaction.

"Are you shocked?" she asked.

"No. I'm not that old-fashioned. Why didn't you say anything? And what does Miguel say about the two of us?"

"You didn't ask. He doesn't say anything about us."

"But why the blatant unfaithfulness? Can't you get a divorce? Is that it?"

"No, we were married in a civil ceremony. We could easily get a divorce if we wanted to."

"But you don't want to?"

"There's no reason to. We aren't married in the traditional sense." She was playing with her lighter. It looked like she wanted more coffee and was cursing the fact that her cup was just as empty as the restaurant. My meeting with the policeman was approaching, and I was impatient.

"I don't get it."

"It's not that complicated. No more complicated than anything else in this town. I married Miguel when he was in prison. Our wedding night lasted ten minutes; we were allowed to talk to each other in a room with the door open. Outside there was a prison guard keeping an eye on what we were doing. It was humiliating."

"I can understand that."

"No you can't," she said angrily. "What do you know about our situation? What do you as a man know about a woman's situation? Before we had our pathetic few minutes together, I had to take off all my clothes and a female gorilla searched me both inside and out as if I were some kind of junkie whore."

I reached across the table and took her hand. Played with her fingers, caressed her wrist. Felt like kissing her.

She sighed, as if she couldn't decide whether she should tell me or forget about it. Then she said, "I wanted to have a bond with Miguel, but it was also a political act. The prisoners had been on a hunger strike, and to punish them the authorities decided to send them to a prison way down south in Andalusia. There is an old prison there. It's about as far away from home as you can get." She let go of my hand and signaled toward where the waitresses were standing waiting for us to finish. But they didn't seem impatient, and Ogoya got a brandy without any trouble. I stuck with mineral water and a little wine.

"It wasn't enough that they sent them all the way down to Puerto de Santa María. They also denied them visits from anyone except their immediate family — parents, children, and wives. Miguel's parents are poor. They work hard in the mountains. It was a long and expensive trip for them to take, and here in Spain it's the family who keeps the prisoners properly clothed and fed and makes life tolerable for them."

"So that's why you married Miguel?"

"Not just because of that, but it was one of the reasons. In principle I'm against marriage. But I loved him, and I still do. He's the person I'm closest to." The brandy arrived, and she took a long swallow.

"But after we got married I had the rights of a wife, and that helped Miguel. He was very depressed, and I was depressed too because of the breakup with Paxti."

"Paxti?"

"Paxti was my lover when I was very young. He brought me down from the mountains. I can't say that I was in love with him — I was obsessed with him. That's the way Paxti is. There's something about him that makes women fall for him, and fall hard. Of course he cheated on me as soon as he had the chance. I was young and deeply hurt the first time. The second time I was on the verge of suicide. The third time it was still awful. By the tenth time it was bearable."

She drank the last of her brandy.

"So you were involved in the whole period we were just talking about?"

She smiled. "How do you think I was involved?"

I looked at her, uncomprehending, so she continued.

"I'm a woman, Poul. I thought you had discovered that. I was involved. I licked stamps, typed, and made coffee for the

warriors." Her laughter took the edge off the sharpness in her
voice.

"No," she said, "that's not completely true. Those were hard
years, but the men want to romanticize them today. We women
haven't reached that point yet, but we've been killed and
maimed and martyred too. Someday we'll write our story."

We sat in silence for a while.

"You said that your marriage to Miguel wasn't traditional.
What did you really mean by that?" I asked.

"It started off pretty weird, don't you think? Paxti split for
France; I went after him, but he threw me out. He didn't want
to have anything to do with me. He was drunk and he felt guilty
because his father's money had saved him. He told me to get the
hell out of there, to go take care of Miguel."

"Are you still a little in love with Paxti?"

"He was hard to get over."

"So then what happened?"

"I started visiting Miguel in prison as often as I could. It was
easy for us to talk to each other. He has always been a rather
silent, reserved type, but that's just on the surface. And we had
so much in common. We grew up in the same environment,
and together we tried to figure out what that had done to us. We
had a disadvantage compared to other people, but we had also
learned some values that we rediscovered together."

She leaned toward me. "Then something strange happened."

"What was that?"

"I discovered that I couldn't live without him."

"But you had never even been to bed with him."

"What does that have to do with it?" she asked angrily.

"Ogoya. I know what it's like to be with you."

There was a slightly awkward silence.

"You're right. It has a lot to do with it. But it didn't back
then. Miguel was almost beaten to death. If he hadn't been so

strong, both physically and mentally, he would have been a
vegetable. But he was still a human being. He learned to function as well as anyone could after such a terrible experience.
You and I can't imagine what it must be like to live with that."

"No, we can't," I said. Her grayish-green eyes were moist.
There were fine little wrinkles at the corners of her eyes and a
hint of some near her mouth, but again I was struck by how
unlined and young her face was. She had an open face, sensitive
to pain and happiness behind that moody, silent shell.

"You couldn't have sex in prison anyway, you know," she
said.

"But he was in prison for years!"

"So you want to know if I had any lovers?"

I nodded.

"A few. Not many. Paxti was the first one, and for a long
time no one could take his place. But I looked. That's true."

"What did Miguel say?"

"We didn't talk about it. We didn't talk about sex."

"But then he got out."

"Yes, and we were alone together, but nothing came of it.
They smashed something inside him. They must have, even
though the doctors can't find anything physically wrong. But we
sleep together once in a while because it's comfortable. Miguel
doesn't talk about his feelings on that subject. We both lead our
own lives."

I sat there staring at her. Totally absorbed. Her face was on
the verge of dissolving in tears even though she managed to
control the trembling that was spreading from her feet all the
way up through her body. Again I took her hands and leaned
over the table to kiss her. I wanted to kiss her gently, like a
brother, but she pulled one hand free and put it around my
neck; she pressed her lips hard against mine. It didn't feel good.
It was unpleasant, and I had to fight the urge to resist and pull

my head away. Finally she let me go, and I sat back in my chair. We filled the silence with more cigarettes. Tobacco is a godsend for covering up awkward silences and uncomfortable situations.

"So you don't live together?" I asked.

"No. We usually live separately. But we see each other a lot. At least once a day. As I told you before, I love him."

That made me feel bad, but I still laughed.

"Do you think that's funny?" she asked.

"It's because I was thinking that when I met Miguel the first time I was sure he was Charlotte's Basque lover."

Now it was Ogoya's turn to take my hand. She had that smile again — the one with a streak of malice in it.

"She probably gave it a try."

Of course I knew it was true — I knew how Charlotte was. But the remark still made jealousy race through my body. And again I recognized the vague feeling of rage that had gripped me during our life together. But before the rage and jealousy could take over and self-pity make its appearance, it struck me again that now I was a free man. She couldn't play her games with me or hurt me anymore.

"She probably did," was all I said.

"Are all Danish men like you?" Ogoya asked.

"What am I like?"

"Forgiving."

"Are all Spanish men like Miguel?"

"Miguel isn't a Spaniard, he's Basque. And nobody is like Miguel."

"I can see that."

Now there was a definite coolness between us.

"Do you know what?" she said, pulling her hands away.

"No, what?"

"Paxti might have been La Danesa's lover."

"Are you trying to hurt me? Or are you just teasing me?"

She made little sounds with her mouth like a mother shushing a baby. It made me furious, and I wished that I could pull myself together, leave the table, and slam the door. But the bill wasn't paid yet; my upbringing prevented me from evading an obligation. My down-to-earth sense of reality once again took the melodrama out of my life.

"I'm just teasing you a little, Poul," she said, taking my hand again. Sunshine returned to the table. "But there might have been something between them. Think about it. Who's after you, Poul?"

"And why are they after me?"

Of course I had thought about that, but I hadn't reached any conclusions. So instead I skirted the subject.

"Maybe Paxti was just like Claes," I said.

"In what way?"

"He could get any woman he wanted."

For the first time she laughed out loud, breaking the tension, and I laughed along with her.

"Are we fourteen-year-olds, or what?" I said.

"Claes can get a certain type of woman who falls for his, shall we say, robust Nordic charm. Paxti is a conqueror," she said in a serious voice. "First he possesses your body, and then your soul. Like a poisonous spider he grabs hold of you, and you can't get rid of him again."

"Aren't there any pictures of Paxti?" I asked.

She gave me a quizzical look.

"Claes met Paxti. The man from the embassy in Madrid. Shouldn't Claes have recognized him?"

She hesitated.

"There are some pictures, but they're old and of very poor quality. And he has a full beard in them. I don't think Claes has ever met Paxti. Claes met Miguel for the first time a few years ago. After the breakup."

"But they seem like old friends."

"They're like an old married couple. They can't stand each other, but they can't do without each other either, or their endless fights."

"I'd like to meet Paxti," I said.

"What do you mean? You *have* met him," said Ogoya.

"Yes, but he was playing a role — the role of the embassy official. I'd like to see him the way he really is."

"Actually I think everything is a role for Paxti. The role he has played the longest is the revolutionary. And now the show has run so long it can't be taken off the marquee. There aren't any other plays left for Paxti."

"He pushed me in the water, you know. That's one way of introducing yourself. A lot has happened in the last few days. It's not like the life I normally lead."

"Tell me a little about that."

So I did. She listened with interest. How much interest, I don't know, but at any rate with open, lively eyes. I told her about my children and my life part-time at home and part-time at work. While I was talking I missed my kids more than ever.

Finally we left. Ogoya dropped me off in front of the Police Commissariat by the city hall. It was a squat building with the Spanish flag waving overhead and two officers with bulletproof vests and submachine guns in front of the door.

I didn't feel all that good about the situation. I felt sick at the thought of being confronted with Charlotte's remains. A face blown up and burned beyond recognition. Maybe I could get out of identifying her. The mixture of sorrow and relief hadn't abated. Both emotions were battling inside me, waiting for the resolution that might bring understanding.

"When are we going to see each other again?" I asked Ogoya.

"Soon."

"This might be our last evening and night together," I insisted.

"Here we say: It's never the last. It's always the next-to-last."

"Stop being childish. Take me seriously."

She was almost the same height as me, so she only had to stretch a little to give me a fleeting kiss.

"Ciao," she said and left. The two policemen were watching her undulating hips in the tight jeans, and she knew it. A little way down the street she did a very elegant and very sexy bump with her hip, and without turning around she waved back at us three men, standing there with our mouths open.

12

The police commissioner was a small man in his fifties with a kindly, bland face in the process of decay. I had expected him to be in uniform. Claes had said that the police in Spain were controlled by officers from the army. He was in civilian clothes but looked like a man who would feel at home in the officers' mess sporting his medals. His office was plain, with a large desk, a view of an ugly courtyard, and pictures on the wall of the Spanish royal couple, who were dressed much too gaudily and had their gaze fixed on a point somewhere near infinity. The only extravagance in his office was a battery of telephones lined up along his desk. The door to his office was covered in thick brown leather. The Spanish flag stood in the corner.

"My condolences. I'm very sorry. Please accept the deepest sympathy of myself and my staff. May God bless her soul and may He help the motherless children. Won't you sit down?" He spoke clear English with a heavy accent.

"Thank you. You speak excellent English," I said in my halting Spanish.

"And you speak excellent Spanish. Shall we converse in that language?"

"I prefer English," I said.

"*Så vi tale engelsk. Jeg ikke tale dansk særlig godt,*" he said with a smile. His upper lip was covered by a little mustache. Covered is just the right word for it — it looked like it was glued on.

He obviously enjoyed my surprised reaction at hearing the broken Danish.

"You're surprised," he said in English. "Some years ago I spent a good deal of time at the embassy both in your country and in Sweden. Wonderful countries. Cold, but quite efficient. Well-developed, with general social harmony. But cold for someone from the South. Would you like to smoke?" He offered me a box of cigarettes both with and without filter.

I took one without a filter. He got up from his desk and lit it for me before I managed to find my own matches. His cufflinks looked like gold. He sat down again.

"I didn't know that police officers were employed at the embassies," I said.

"Well, police officers — that means so many things. All democratic countries are concerned with security problems. The unfortunate spread of international terrorism requires extraordinary countermeasures, don't you agree?" He blew the smoke up toward the ceiling. It seemed to be a habit with him. Every time he took a drag he leaned his head back like a rooster drinking and let the smoke climb upwards.

If he had been in Denmark and Sweden a number of years ago, it would have been during the dictatorship, and that meant he was probably there to keep an eye on the enemies of the regime in the exile communities. Charlotte would probably have made an issue of it in sharp, well-turned phrases; but that wasn't my concern, after all, so I just nodded . . . as usual, you might say.

"Your wife — may God have mercy on her soul — was interested in these matters, wasn't she?"

"In what matters?"

"International terrorism."

"She wrote about it. Did TV programs on it. She was a journalist."

"Yes, where would international terrorism be without the press? I often think, if we clamped a lid on news of all terrorist activity for one year, wouldn't we achieve the desired result? A terrorist with no publicity really doesn't have any purpose, does he?"

Politics again. I didn't want to talk about it.

"You can't tell a free press what to write," I said just to say something, no matter how banal it was.

"A free press is not the same as an irresponsible press. But journalists do what they feel like, I suppose. You're not a journalist, are you, Mr. Jensen?"

"No. I'm a jurist."

"An attorney, I see." I didn't have the energy to explain the difference.

He laid his head back again and exhaled toward the ceiling.

"There are no problems. Your embassy has taken care of the practical end. You may pick up the body tomorrow morning. It will be in a zinc coffin. You will have no trouble transporting it to Madrid and on to Denmark."

Just like that. Completely matter-of-fact. It sounded brutal to me, but what are you going to say? I said thanks.

"This is nothing new," he said. "All too often I've had to send my people out of here in zinc coffins to some sun-baked village in Andalusia."

"I'm sorry."

"The fatherland demands many sacrifices of those who have chosen the path of duty."

"You're probably right. Could I see my wife now?"

"Of course. I have been clumsy. Forgive me."

I was captured by his style and spread my hands in what was meant as an evasive maneuver, a gesture of forgiveness.

He said, "Permit me one more question about your wife's work. Did she have connections in the world of international terrorism?"

"I don't understand."

"I don't mean literally, of course, but a journalist often has to go straight to the source."

"I have no idea."

He smiled and leaned forward on his elbows and patted his hands together. His nails were manicured. He had a large gold watch on his left wrist and rings on both hands.

"No," he said. "There was no reason to kill her."

"I don't understand."

"No." He leaned back once more. "You don't know what your wife was doing in that bar?"

"I was several thousand kilometers away."

"I know. The Nordic countries. So liberal, so progressive, so modern." There was no doubt about the irony in his voice, though he maintained his friendly, slightly smiling expression.

"I don't understand," I said for the third time.

"No," he said. "I don't either."

"What don't you understand?"

"What your wife was doing in that bar."

"Drinking a cup of coffee. How should I know?"

He laughed.

"*Touché!* An obvious explanation. Forgive an old policeman who sees conspiracies everywhere."

"Well, that wasn't the only bomb that ever went off here in San Sebastián."

He spread his arms wide. Everything about him was exaggerated, theatrical.

"So true, so true. Unfortunately not everyone is willing to accept our democratic way of life."

I was starting to get really annoyed.

"You're not sitting there saying that my wife was involved in all that?"

"Was she?"

"No, damn it! The Danish police were on the same track. It's totally impossible. It's absurd."

"Be assured, my friend, that nothing in this world is impossible. Listen to the words of an old policeman. A man who has seen it all. A man who isn't surprised by anything." He paused. "Besides, a moment ago you said that you didn't know what your wife was doing, didn't you?"

"She was a journalist, not a terrorist. You see spooks in broad daylight."

"If only I did." His voice was harder now. "Spooks don't send my people home in zinc coffins. Spooks don't threaten the Spanish state. Terrorists do."

"My wife didn't."

"Certainly no one is implying that she did, Mr. Jensen."

"I'm glad to hear that."

"Our task is to clear up the details. You understand that, I presume?"

I nodded. He got up.

"Now for the identification. Then you will receive her effects," he said.

I got up too. There was a moment of confusion before we figured out how to get through the door in the proper order. He led the way and I followed; we went down a linoleum corridor with bare, mud-colored walls. After hearing Miguel's story I felt uneasy being there. It was as if the hidden screams were inside the walls and the most horrible secrets could be found behind each and every office door.

We waited by the elevator. We hadn't said anything on the way. The police commissioner was not much taller than me. He had a strong but discreet odor of expensive cologne.

"Aside from these regrettable circumstances, have you otherwise had a pleasant stay in our country?" he asked.

"Yes, fine, thank you. The Basque country has excellent cuisine."

"That is one compensation of being stationed up here, I must admit."

He pressed the elevator button a couple of times. It finally lit up and there was a rumble behind the door. There was nobody in the elevator when the sliding doors opened. I went in first, and he pressed a button that said *Baja*, and we went down. The elevator moved in tiny, barely perceptible jerks that almost made me sick to my stomach. I was sweating and could feel the drops trickling down from my armpits all the way to my belt. It wasn't even very warm, and when I had left the restaurant with Ogoya the air had been full of a salty sea breeze off the bay. I was desperate for a smoke but didn't dare light up.

The elevator stopped with a bump. The police commissioner smiled apologetically and the door opened. His eyes were expressionless and his skin showed no trace of sweat. There were nicotine stains along the edge of his mustache.

"So you probably don't know very many people here in San Sebastián," he said for no reason as we stepped out into a narrow corridor with naked yellow walls and a tile floor. It was cold, and the light glared harshly from bare bulbs surrounded by steel mesh. It wasn't the damp cold you associate with dungeons and lonely cells, but a dry, almost hospital-like cold that gave the impression of efficiency, cleanliness, and order. It was a very un-Spanish atmosphere.

"No. I haven't had a chance to meet anybody."

"A couple of lonesome days."

"You might say that."

"It's said that chance acquaintances can lend spice to a journey."

"Yes, they can," I said, with a suspicion of what he was leading up to. But he let it drop.

"This way, Mr. Jensen," was all he said.

We went down the corridor and came to a steel door. He rang a bell and we waited again.

"Did you come to San Sebastián by air?" he asked. "It's a hair-raising landing in that little prop plane."

"I wouldn't know. I came by car," I said. If only he would shut up. My stomach was tying itself in knots.

"Many people are afraid to fly. That's quite natural. The unnatural thing is not to be afraid. A barbaric way to travel, don't you think?"

"I wouldn't know. I got a ride with someone." Why wasn't somebody coming to open that damned door? The corridor divided into two a little farther down, I could see. There were a lot of doors, both regular and steel ones. It was completely quiet. I was expecting any second that the silence would be shattered by a tortured scream, a plea for help. And I was sure that the police commissioner wouldn't raise either of his well-trimmed eyebrows if that happened.

"I thought you said you didn't know anybody," he said. He didn't ring the bell again. My fingers were itching to do it myself so we could get it over with.

"It was a chance meeting."

"I see. Another attorney?"

"One of Charlotte's colleagues. A chance encounter on the plane to Madrid. I thought it would be nice to have some company on the way up here."

"That's understandable. A journalist, eh?"

I nodded. Wasn't that door ever going to open?

"They appear like vultures around a dying animal."

"Pardon?"

"Journalists. They come at the first sign of trouble, which grows as soon as they land, screeching and cackling."

"You're putting the cart before the horse," I said in Danish, and I wanted to add: you fascist pig, but remembered that he had lived in Denmark and Sweden. I held back the words in time.

"I don't understand . . ." he said. "Unfortunately, my Danish . . ."

"It was just nonsense," I said in English.

He looked at me, puzzled. A little inquisitively, as if he

didn't find the moment particularly suited to nonsense, even
though he was the one who insisted on keeping up the small
talk.

How would Charlotte look? Would there only be pieces of
her left? Would she be burned beyond recognition? Would she
smell? Would her eyes be open or closed? Would he expect me
to touch her? Maybe even kiss her on the forehead? My hands
started shaking, and finally a bolt was pulled back and the door
opened.

A uniformed policeman with a rubber apron over his fat
stomach said hello matter-of-factly, and we entered a tiled room
with a row of square gray hatches along the back wall and a large
table in the middle. The room was very sterile and very cold.
Still, the fat policeman looked like he was sweating. He was very
big and had a square, ruddy face and smelled of black tobacco
and liquor. He didn't say anything, just stood looking expectantly at his boss, who nodded. The fat man pulled out one of
the drawers. There was a white sheet over the bundle, which
looked small, stunted, and defenseless. As though it were only a
child lying there. Then the police commissioner lifted the sheet
just enough to reveal half of her face. The other half was gone.
But it was Charlotte lying there, cold and blue and white and
stiff and utterly still.

"Is that the kind of people you want to help — people who
do things like this?" said the police commissioner with no kindness in his voice, but no harshness or anger either. I wanted
badly to turn my head away from the sight in front of me, but I
couldn't tear myself away. Why didn't he let go of the sheet and
cover her back up? Why didn't he send that lump back to the
hole in the wall where it came from? He just stood there with his
Spanish contempt for death, and I was almost hypnotized.
I could have just looked away, pulled my eyes away. But I kept
standing there for what felt like a lifetime, yet it was only a few
seconds.

"I'll ask you again, Mr. Jensen. What was your wife doing in that bar at precisely that moment?" Now his voice was hard, and it tore me out of my spell so I was able to turn my head away from the remains of Charlotte's face.

"I don't know," I said in a whisper.

"Look at her!" he snapped, and I felt an iron-hard hand grab the back of my neck and force my face down toward Charlotte's. It was the fat policeman, who now stood right in back of me. I was sweating so hard I was sopping wet, and my stomach convulsed.

"What was she doing in the bar?"

"What's the big idea? I don't know. Let go of me at once." My voice wouldn't get any louder. Still just a whisper, which made no impression in the cold tiled room, where our breath swirled like fog.

"What was she doing there?"

"I don't know. What difference does it make?" I said in a whisper.

Now he shouted so loudly and so close to my ear that I could feel his spit like fine drops against my cheek just above the edge of my beard. I was more terrified than I had ever been in my life. It was the second time in twenty-four hours that someone had laid a hand on me.

"What was she doing in the bar? Tell me!"

"I don't know."

"You're lying!"

"No I'm not. Why is it so important?"

"Because two of my best men were killed by that bomb. Two years' work getting close to the center of that damned terrorist gang was blown to smithereens along with them. So I'll ask you one more time: What was your wife doing in the bar?"

I tried to tear myself free, but it was impossible. I was soaking wet with sweat and my heart was pounding, and a few inches from my eyes was the most horrifying sight I had ever seen.

"I don't know," I said. I had gotten my voice back. It was whining, and I was on the verge of tears.

"I don't know," I repeated. "Good God, my wife was killed too. She was there by accident. I don't know."

He let the sheet fall over Charlotte's face and shoved the slab back into the hole in the wall. The grip on my neck was released, and I cautiously tried to straighten up. The fat man's hand was gone and I could stand up straight now. I took a step back and to the side to get away from him. The fat man stood by the table with his legs spread in the military at-ease position; his face was expressionless. He still hadn't said anything but hello. Now I wanted to get out of there, but he was standing between me and the door.

"A cigarette, Mr. Jensen," said the police commissioner, holding out the pack. I nodded, but I almost couldn't fish one out, my hands were shaking so hard. He lit mine first, then his own.

"You see, Mr. Jensen," he said in a friendly tone, but with eyes as cold as the tiled room, "there are so many things I don't understand. And that makes me sad."

"I would like to get out of here."

"You will when we're finished talking."

"You can't keep me here."

"I can do whatever I want with you. With the anti-terrorism law in my hand I can keep you in custody for ten days without a soul needing to know about it."

He was probably right. I was more terrified than I had ever been before. I was glad that I didn't know anything. That I couldn't betray or turn in anyone, because there was no one to betray. I would have made a pitiful freedom fighter.

"I don't believe you can keep me here. And I'm going to report your behavior to the Danish embassy. I'm not just some

Spaniard you can mistreat any way you want," I managed to say.

He laughed, cackling like a bantam rooster.

"Nonsense. There are no witnesses. And we haven't laid a finger on you. Now let's just have a little talk."

Even down here he exhaled the smoke by laying his head back and blowing it up toward the ceiling.

"I don't know a thing," I said.

"Wouldn't you like to get hold of the people who murdered your wife?"

"Of course I would."

"Then why are you hanging around with the terrorist gang that's behind this mess?"

"What do you mean?"

"Hylander. Miguel. Ogoya... do those names mean any-thing to you?"

Once again I was shaken. .

"You've been having me followed."

"You haven't answered my question."

"They aren't terrorists," I said.

He laughed again. "Just because they were released in order to pacify soft-hearted international opinion does not change the fact that Miguel Boyer has been sentenced for terrorist activity and that his wife Ogoya has assisted him and that Mr. Hylander has always supported the cause of international communism in his writings."

For the first time he looked as if he might lose his compo-sure. The spit flew from the corners of his mouth, and he had taken a step toward me. But his rage actually calmed my nerves. Now I suddenly saw him as the lackey he was — a loser who had watched his world collapse when democracy was introduced. A dinosaur who had survived on the southern tip of Europe.

Miguel had put his guns on the shelf because he had won the fight; that's exactly how simple it was.

There was something else I suddenly understood.

"You were the one who interrogated Miguel back then. Weren't you?"

"I met him in Madrid. That's correct."

"So you're a torturer."

Again he laughed. "If nothing else, terrorists can always yell about torture if they can't get sympathy on their side any other way. That's an old trick. But do they think about the suffering, the torture they inflict on those left behind when they shoot and bomb my people? Isn't that a violation of human rights too? Thou shalt not kill," he quoted in conclusion.

I was feeling even better now.

"Then we have nothing more to discuss," I said.

He looked me up and down, slowly, as he would a woman.

"Not today," he said. "But another day, perhaps."

"Couldn't we find someplace else to meet?"

"There's one more thing. It's about a man they call Paxti. Do you know him?"

"I know of him."

"But you have never met him?"

"Sort of."

"What do you mean?"

"I would really like to tell you everything I know. But only on the condition that we get out of here." This place scared me to death, which he could obviously see.

The police commissioner looked at me for a long time with his expressionless eyes.

"It's a deal," he said, surprisingly.

"And I don't want to be threatened in the future," I added recklessly.

He looked at me for quite a while before he spoke.

"That won't be necessary anyway." Then he nodded to the fat policeman, who pulled back the bolt. I had to stop myself from breaking into a run. I politely followed the police commissioner out. The fat man stayed behind.

We went over to the elevator. It was waiting. He ushered me in with a polite gesture, but he stayed outside. I was still shaken and felt myself in his power when he said sternly:

"Poul Jensen, listen carefully and don't interrupt." His hand blocked the automatic doors so they wouldn't close. "Go immediately to the officer at the front desk and get your passport back by turning in your visitor's ID card." He pointed at the plastic card fastened by a little clip to my lapel.

"I don't understand . . ."

"Stop interrupting me."

He glanced down the hallway as if checking to see that we were still alone.

"Then go straight to your friends, Miguel and Hylander. Got it?"

I nodded.

"Tell them this: The Fish wants company at the funeral. Repeat!"

"The Fish wants company at the funeral."

"Do it at once!"

He released the door and it started to close. I wanted to protest, but he didn't let me speak.

"Now, right away!" he said with a tense expression on his face, as the door closed and the elevator rose up from the cellar.

13

*H*alf an hour later I was still dazed, and my clothes felt sweaty and grimy. I was sitting in Claes' hotel room with my second whiskey in my hand, poured neat from a duty-free bottle. The room faced the bay, and it was dark outside. The island was visible only as a shadow, like a delicate paper cutout in the gray, swelling sea. There were a lot of people on the promenade. They were taking their evening stroll even though the weather was threatening to change; the air had turned humid. Heavy clouds were scudding in from the ocean in a steady stream.

Miguel was there too. He was drinking mineral water and smoking his black cigarettes. He was sitting on the bed, while Claes sat at a kind of nightstand with his typewriter in front of him. There was a sheet of paper in it. He had been working when I came rushing in with my story. Now I had calmed down.

"And what exactly did he say?" Claes asked again.

"The Fish wants company at the funeral."

"Did he say it in Spanish?"

"No, in English!"

"The Fish wants company at the funeral. Do you know what it means?"

"I don't have the slightest idea." A thought suddenly occurred to me. "Ogoya said something earlier about a sardine that's going to be buried."

Claes laughed. I could see him double, from the front and

from the back. He was sitting in front of a mirror. It must be odd to sit and type while you're staring yourself in the face.

"That's right. For the finale to the carnival, they're going to bury a giant papier-mâché sardine on the beach tonight. That's why there are so many people dressed in black on the street. They're mourning the burial of the carnival."

"What do you mean by 'bury'?"

"It's like your St. Hans bonfire. They set all that shit on fire."

"And then what?"

"Then it's over and people keep on drinking and tomorrow everything goes back to normal."

"Show him!" said Miguel. We'd almost forgotten him sitting there on the bed with a cigarette in his hand, and the ghastly memories inside his head that weren't visible on his face.

Claes dug into the front of his shirt and pulled out a thin bag he had on a chain around his neck. He unzipped it and fished out a piece of paper. It was plain white and neatly folded. He got up and handed it to me and sat down again. It was typed in Spanish. After I read it I was even more confused.

"Do you understand it?" asked Claes, taking a gulp of whiskey. He waved his hand to ask whether I wanted any more. I shook my head. He poured himself a couple of fingers.

"I understand the words, if that's what you mean. But not the content."

It said: "The Danish journalist Charlotte Damsborg (La Danesa in San Sebastián) died today because I decided she should die. At my request, her husband wants company at the funeral. The Fish."

"That's pretty weird," I said.

"The weirdest part is that Miguel and I got exactly the same message on exactly the same day. Miguel here in San Sebastián.

Me in Stockholm. And the weirdest thing of all is that we got the message the day before Charlotte was killed."

I was furious. "Why the hell didn't you tell me this before?"

He kept his cool.

"Because there was a catch." He took another drink. "I was supposed to keep my mouth shut for at least five days, and then I would get a scoop that would make me rich and famous."

"And you fell for that?"

"Wouldn't you? What did I have to lose?"

"So that's why you looked for me on the plane?"

"No, that was a coincidence. I didn't get away the day before because of a strike in Stockholm. I figured I wouldn't meet you until I got here."

"You're a real shithead!"

"What did I have to lose, Poul? Do you think it's been easy keeping my mouth shut?"

"You poor jerk."

If only I wasn't so tired. There had been something happening all the time. It had been impossible to relax for even a minute. And the lack of sleep. The alcohol. Ogoya. The endless lies. I didn't even have time to think.

"There's one more thing," said Claes.

"Don't tell me Charlotte's still alive," I sneered.

Claes smiled his broad, almost angelic smile, full of sympathy and warmth. That was rare. Usually his smile was all toothpaste and no emotion.

"There's no hope of that, I'm afraid. You saw her dead yourself."

"Then what?"

"Miguel has his fingers in lots of things, as you know. He called me less than ten days ago with some information he said was important. He said that what we all were afraid of was about to happen, and that he was almost certain the code word was 'the Fish.' "

"I don't understand a word you're saying."

"They're planning a military coup, Poul. The code name is 'the Fish.' The leader is called the Sardine, and if they're not stopped in time, there's going to be a bloodbath here."

"What did Charlotte have to do with it?" I should have asked: What am I doing here? I'm a father, a part-time jurist; my world is a walk along the lakes in Copenhagen and a long sleepy afternoon spent in Fælledpark with my kids. In my world the word "coup" belongs in the papers and on TV. That flickering tube had done it again — poisoned our lives, mine and the children's.

"Maybe Charlotte had gotten wind of the plan," said Claes.

"It seems like everybody knows something about it," I said.

"Miguel says no. Miguel says there have been a lot of smoke screens, but this time it's for real."

"Paxti!" I said.

"We don't know anything for sure," said Claes. Miguel had glanced up when I shouted Paxti's name. Otherwise he sat motionless, even though I had the impression he was listening and trying to understand our Scandinavian.

"Who's supposed to be behind it?" I asked.

"The usual powers that see their lives threatened by democracy, by a socialist government, by autonomy, by the new age."

"Why don't you go to the police, to the authorities, and tell them what you know?"

"Because we can't trust anyone in this country. Because the people who have been charged with protecting the democracy are the ones who are the biggest threat."

I shook my head.

"But the police commissioner who gave me that strange message — isn't he one of them? One of those who want the dictatorship back? It's funny, but I got the feeling that he was involved in interrogating Miguel that time in Madrid."

Claes nodded.

"He was." He translated what I had said, and Miguel smiled his beautiful smile.

"Jaime García Monterales. A real bastard if there ever was one," Miguel said.

"What does he want with you?"

"I don't know."

"What *do* you know?" I roared, jumping up.

"Not much yet," he said. I felt like hitting him. He didn't so much as blink. Claes hadn't moved either. I calmed down again. Also because I realized that their silence might be just a cover for insecurity, confusion, and fear. Maybe they didn't know what the next step ought to be either.

But there were still some things I wondered about, even in my foggy condition.

"I don't understand," I said in Spanish, slowly but correctly. "I don't understand, Miguel. How do you know so much? You're just a journalist; you're not a partisan anymore."

"My friend," he said, "you're right. I know more than I should. I know a lot of people. I'm friends with the people who rule Spain now, even though they're Spaniards. Because they are democrats. I trust them. They trust me."

He stopped, got up from the bed, went over to the window, and looked out across the black ocean. The shutters were part-way open and the sea roared, powerful and tender — a peaceful, gentle, pleasant sound.

"I've been the go-between these past few weeks. The intermediary between the government and the people still using guns. We are close to a solution, to a peace agreement. But as often happens, there are strong fascist forces that don't want us to find a solution."

He smiled and took a few steps toward me. He was going to great lengths to make me understand what he was saying. It was a long speech for him. Usually he didn't say much.

"You see, Poul, democracy here is like an egg. It's thin and fragile. The protective covering isn't any stronger than an egg-shell. It would take very little to break it. During these years the egg is cooking, and with every day that passes it gets stronger and stronger. By the time it's hard-boiled we won't have to worry so much about it breaking. Then it will be strong."

"I see what you mean, but what are you getting at?"

"What I'm getting at is that some months ago the government began to suspect that a new coup was in the works. Only a lot bigger and a lot more dangerous than Tejero's comic-opera attempt. But was it anything more than rumors? And what should we, what should the government do? We couldn't trust anyone completely, could we? The people in the security forces? Unreliable. The military? Unreliable. And the government had come to power so recently that the whole bureaucracy was hostile too. What should they do?"

"I don't know."

"The government didn't know either. But one of the things they did was to use me and other people to gather intelligence. To try to find out if we could pry up a little corner of the conspiracy. I've never met my contact here in Euskadi; I've only known him by the name 'the Fish.' "

"You didn't know he was the police commissioner?"

"I don't think anything in my life has ever surprised me more than that he was the one who gave you that message."

"What does it mean?"

"That he is either who he says he is and needs us to act now . . ."

"Or?"

"Or that the conspiracy has gone so far that we can't do anything else. Either way he's going to be a busy man."

He looked genuinely sad about it. There was an air of weari-ness and futility about him, even though his black eyes shone

with the fire I had learned to recognize and admire, though I
didn't know what was behind it.

But I still wasn't satisfied.

"Excuse me," I said in Spanish to Miguel and then switched
over to Danish.

"Isn't it about time you told me what you know? What is
your role?"

Claes looked at me.

"Messenger boy," he said after a pause.

I didn't say anything, so he went on.

"The socialists in the government down here need help.
Officially they have everything under control, of course. They
can't use official channels. They have to make a show of
strength, but they have good connections with the social democrats in Scandinavia. I've carried money and information and
advice between the two groups."

"Why did they pick you?"

"Because my father was a minister in the social democratic
government. I've been a member of the party my whole life.
I know Spain better than any other journalist you could name.
I have plenty of official reasons to come here often." He said
this without bragging, without the self-promotion that usually
marked much of his style. It was a simple answer to a simple
question.

"And Charlotte?"

"For God's sake, Poul, I don't know! As far as I know she
wasn't directly involved in it."

"But you don't know the whole story either, do you?"

"Far from it. We're moving in a twilight world here. There's
no true or false. It's nothing but rumors and speculation; suspicion is the name of the game. We're all waiting and watching
each other, afraid of who's going to make the next move."

Over the crashing of the surf the sound of funeral music

came from far off. Slow and wailing, with muffled drums that set the pace, driving the flutes and brass instruments. I went out onto the little balcony. Claes and Miguel followed and stood right behind me. The air was fresh and salty. The sea was now gray, with heavy swells; the sand shone like white gold in the glow of the streetlamps. It was crowded with people along the railing and on the promenade. Up near the old casino we could see the procession appear. In the front they were carrying a huge, grayish fish. After them came the band, and then the rest of the people, in a sinuous procession.

They were all dressed in black; they moved slowly up toward the hotel, impelled by the melancholy call of the music.

"What is it?" I asked.

"*El entierro de la sardina*," said Claes.

"Yes," said Miguel, "it's time. We're going to meet our Fish."

It would have to be the Fish who met *us*, found us in the crowds on the promenade, because how would we ever find him?

Now you could tell it was February. It was cold, but in a fresh, clear way, like an early fall day on the Danish coast. I would have liked to call home, but Claes and Miguel wanted to leave right away, so I gave up the idea.

By the time we got downstairs the music had grown louder, and now you could hear that the people in the procession were singing. The words disintegrated in the wind and blew away, but that didn't matter. It was both funeral music and festival music at the same time. Again it was the drums that we heard. The same muffled carnival rhythm as before, but a beat slower; it seemed clearer and it cut right to your soul.

The fish looked gigantic, like an enormous boat with teeth and papier-mâché fins and a body of wood. It was painted gray and green like a sardine, and it was being carried by men and

women dressed in black with their faces covered. The people in
the procession behind it were also dressed in black. Their faces
were masked or painted white and yellow. Many of them wore
hoods, and almost all of them had torches in their hands. The
children shrieked in delight at the eerie sight of the black ghosts
and painted skeletons. We stood there for a while and watched,
then fell into step with the procession and followed along the
rest of the way to the beach.

The fish was slowly and ceremonially carried down the
stairs, right down onto the beach. The torchlight seemed to
grow brighter as the procession and the music moved away from
the lights on the promenade. The wind was still mercilessly
tearing the music to shreds. As usual the island lay out in the
bay like a fuzzy lump under the driving clouds. There was a
floodlight on the foothills to the left, and to the right the figure
of Christ loomed threateningly toward the pagan drama on the
beach.

We didn't go all the way to the edge of the water but stopped
right at the bottom of the steps. Claes and Miguel were moving
their heads from side to side, their eyes scanning the spectators,
looking for some sign that would tell them whether their Fish
had also arrived. I was freezing in my sweater and jacket.
I wished I had gone back to the hotel to get my coat.

The fish was carried all the way out to the water's edge. The
music must have gotten louder or else the wind had died down,
because now we could hear the droning song over the flicker of
the torches again. Miguel tugged at my sleeve, and we walked
together toward the water. The beach was very wide now that
the tide had gone out. The sand was damp and firm. We walked
in our own little procession; first Claes, as usual, like a beacon
with his blond hair, then Miguel, and me bringing up the rear.
Only Ogoya was missing, then it would have been just like that
night during carnival. What had I been looking for that night so

long ago? And had I found it? What were we looking for tonight?
Or, more precisely, who was looking for us?

As we approached the big grayish-green sardine, which lay
there baring its phony teeth, looking almost alive in the torchlight, we could see that it wasn't a real funeral, but a party.
Those who weren't carrying torches had bottles and wineskins in
their hands. Everyone was smiling and laughing, and their eyes
flashed through the masks. The song went on, plaintive and sad.

I jumped when someone slid an arm around my waist, but
my shock turned to joy when I recognized whose arm it was, her
hip against mine, her head on my shoulder, and her eyes
through the domino mask. Ogoya. She gave me her butterfly
kiss, and I expected her to vanish as quickly as she had come,
but she stayed there with one arm around my waist. The beach
was full of people. The air was charged with anticipation.
Collectively we waited for something to happen, for the release
to come.

The song died away. Ogoya ran a few steps forward and
threw her torch in a low, perfect arc over the people dressed in
black and up onto the fish. The torch hit it on the back, sput-
tered, and slid down a bit before it caught. The wood began to
smoulder, but now Ogoya's torch was joined by another one,
and another, and then so many that you couldn't count them
anymore. The crowd couldn't keep up with them either. The
first torches had been greeted with a long, drawn-out "oooooh,"
but now it all dissolved into clamor. The music began again, the
dancing started, and the sardine flared up so its death throes
were clearly mirrored in the gleaming surface of the sea.

Ogoya had come back and put her arm around my waist
again. She had taken off her mask, and her face was glowing.
Her black clothes clung to her body and outlined her curves in
the blazing firelight. Suddenly she stiffened and pulled me
close. I followed her glance; about twenty yards away I saw

Claes, who was standing there watching the burning sardine. A few steps to his right stood Miguel, paralyzed, like a pillar of salt waiting to be freed. Directly to Miguel's left stood a man dressed all in black with a mask hiding his entire face. It looked like they were talking intimately with each other, but now I saw what Ogoya had seen. The man in black was holding something pressed against Miguel's back, an object that made Miguel stand still in the dancing light from the burning carnival fish. They were standing like Siamese twins locked in an involuntary embrace, surrounded by dancing people wearing masks and black clothes, illuminated by flames that were jumping higher and higher into the air so the sparks rained down into the sea.

They stood like that for only a minute or two, then glided apart. I tried to follow the man in black with my eyes, but he merged with the others in the night and was gone, as if someone had spirited him away. Miguel went over to Claes. They talked together for a moment. Claes motioned with his head toward Ogoya and me, and they came over to us.

"That was the Fish," said Miguel without emotion, but his face was twisted into a mask full of hatred.

"So was it the police commissioner?" I asked.

"Yes, it was."

"Are you sure? What about the mask, the disguise?"

"Yes, I'm sure. I listened to that voice for the three longest days of my life. I'll never forget it."

"What did he say?" It was Ogoya who asked. She didn't seem surprised. She had let go of me and instead was standing close to Miguel.

"He wants to have a meeting in an hour. He said it's important. For me. For him. For Spain. Those were his words."

"Where?" asked Ogoya.

Miguel pointed up to one of the foothills.

"Are we going?" I asked.

"He said all four of us should come," said Miguel.

"So are we going?"

"Yes," said Miguel, "we'll go up there and listen to what he has to say."

"That sounds like a good idea," I said.

"And then maybe I'll kill him," said Miguel.

It sounded so simple, and none of us had a thing to say.

14

We got to Miguel's car just as the rain started. I had expected a violent storm, a release after the way the clouds had been building up all day, but it arrived as a fine drizzle that scattered people and sent them into the friendly light of the cafés. The city disappeared below us as the car crawled up the side of the mountain through a series of hairpin curves. In the headlights we could see part of a rough wall, a dark building, and grayish-black trees. No one said a word.

The atmosphere was oppressive and the air was heavy with the smoke of our cigarettes. Ogoya and Miguel had almost gotten into a fight. At a furious speed, Miguel had first driven to a part of town where we hadn't been before. A poorer, more run-down area, without the glitter and smell of wealth I had come to associate with San Sebastián. There were long dark blocks of tenements and only a few small cafés. There were hardly any people on the streets, only the stream of cars going by.

We had stopped at an apartment building, and without a word Miguel had jumped out of the car and disappeared in the entryway. Ogoya was sitting in the back seat of the car with me. Claes was sitting up front, looking the other way. She had said something to Miguel in their incomprehensible language, but he shook his head and snapped at her; she had retreated into silence next to me. I wanted to take her hand, but she had pulled it away.

Now she took mine.

"I hate it," she said in English. "I hate it; we had put it all behind us. Didn't you see what he was doing?"

I shook my head.

She squeezed my hand. "He went to get a gun from one of his friends. I don't want to live that kind of life again. Things were going so well. I don't want to be afraid all the time, afraid of what might happen to him. I don't want to live my life in fear anymore."

"Did you tell him that?"

"He knows that. I told him it was a trap, that they're just out to get him in the slammer again, that they can't stand the thought of him being a free man. It's a trap, I said."

I looked at the back of Miguel's neck and one side of his face in the darkness as the car climbed noisily up the hill. His face had changed. He had the same handsome features, but now there were lines on his face. A tension and concentration that spread all the way down to his hands. But the stress didn't make him nervous the way it did me. Instead he seemed even calmer than before. It was a tense, perilous calm.

"What did Miguel say?" I asked Ogoya.

She snorted and blew smoke at the back of his neck.

"He told me to shut up. Look at him. He loves it. Men! Cops and robbers!"

She pulled her hand away again and huddled in her corner. We had reached the top. Miguel parked the car and turned off the lights. We could hear the rain on the roof, and the light on the dashboard glowed. He had the ignition on so the windshield wipers would keep working. We were parked on a ledge — what looked like a viewpoint. A little higher up we could see a big building, dark and shuttered. We sat there for a while. Miguel stared at the building intently, and I caught sight of the light at the same time he did. It was a flicker, as if someone had lit a cigarette or was holding up a lighter. The glimmer of light was coming from inside the building.

Miguel opened the door. He had his hand in his jacket pocket. The rain blinded me immediately. My glasses were wet and I could hardly see a thing. Claes took me by the arm.

"Hold on to me," he said. "Nothing's going to happen. Miguel knows that. The police commissioner knows that. We've come along as insurance. We're foreigners."

"What kind of building is this?" I asked. My voice was hoarse and I was whispering. The only sound was from the waves, which you could hear crashing at the foot of the mountain. The surf was heavy. It almost drowned out the sound of the raindrops hitting the roof and hood of the car.

"It's a summer restaurant and hotel — closed for the season. It's a popular resort in the summer, but hardly anyone comes here in the winter," said Claes.

We walked up toward the hotel without noticing the rain, which was soaking us, particularly Ogoya, who just had on her black cotton clothes. The rest of us were wearing our windbreakers, but the rain was soon running down the back of my neck anyway. We approached the building up a broad, zigzagging stairway. The steps were worn, and the cement had eroded away in places. We went all the way up to the entrance. A sign in the double glass door said "Closed." After I got under the eaves and cleaned my glasses on a corner of my shirt, I could see that the sign was hanging crooked and the paint was peeling. The foyer inside lay in darkness, and there was no sound but the rain and the surf at the foot of the mountain.

Miguel kept his right hand in his pocket and grabbed the door with his left. It wasn't locked, and it glided open. Inside the lobby a door opened; a strip of light appeared, widening across the floor until the door stopped moving. My heart was hammering and my mouth felt like it was full of dry sand. Miguel walked forward, not cautiously, not stealthily, but with a firm step through the semi-darkness toward the strip of light, and the rest of us followed like ducklings behind their mother.

Our steps echoed in the empty lobby. It was difficult to imagine it in the summer, full of laughter and shouting and suitcases and the smell of sun-tan oil, with a man behind the counter telling the tourists when the next bullfight would be held. We followed Miguel across the waxed floor to the door, which he pulled open all the way before stepping into what looked like a storage room. There were no windows and no furniture. The walls were bare and the floor was cement. It was damp and clammy.

"Please close the door. We wouldn't want to be disturbed by a patrol thinking there's a burglary in progress," said a voice, and I caught sight of the police commissioner. Still in his black clothes, he was leaning against the wall in the far corner. He looked small and weak, and his stomach bulged under the raincoat so he almost looked like a pregnant woman. Like Miguel, he had his right hand in his pocket.

"Good evening," he said.

"Good evening," said Miguel and closed the door.

We waited for him to make the first move. It was a cruel one.

"The last time we met you said that if you ever saw me again you'd kill me."

"I got smarter," said Miguel. "Otherwise I'd have done it."

"I know. That's why the Fish used you. That's why the Fish was able to trust you when he couldn't trust anyone else, Miguel."

Miguel didn't answer. Ogoya and Claes didn't say anything either. It was as if the police commissioner and Miguel were alone in that cold, damp room.

"Allow me to introduce myself," said the police commissioner in the same flat tone and the same polite manner as before. I didn't understand the incredible politeness of Spaniards. It was so often only a mask for the coarsest brutality.

"I am the head of the king's personal security and intelligence service."

I could tell that gave Claes a jolt.

"Yes, you're surprised, Señor Hylander," said the police commissioner. "You have never heard of it before. Formally it doesn't exist. It was established right after the abortive coup in February of 1981. At that time we realized that we couldn't trust either the military or the civilian intelligence services. They were wolves guarding the democratic lamb."

Again he paused. Then he took his right hand out of his pocket, slowly and carefully. In his hand he held a pack of cigarettes and a lighter.

"Why don't we have a smoke," he said.

Miguel took his hand out of his pocket too, and we all lit up. The tension in the room subsided as the aroma of tobacco spread through the damp air.

The police commissioner resumed. "For a long time we have been aware that a new attack on the state was coming, but that this time it would be serious. This time they were determined to succeed, because now they were going to get rid of the greatest obstacle. This time they would assassinate the king and make sure that Basque terrorists got the blame. This assassination would be reason enough for reasonable men to step in and save the country once again. And the USA would understand us, the way the USA always understands anti-communists. The way the USA understood the Turkish generals."

Surprisingly enough it was Claes who spoke.

" 'Us'?" he said.

The police commissioner smiled.

"I told you this time it was serious. I know that because I was one of the people planning the coup."

Miguel's hand slipped back into his right jacket pocket.

"Señor Boyer," said the police commissioner, "that won't be necessary. You have to trust me."

"Why?"

"Because it's your only chance to continue the life you have created for yourself. Because it's the only chance for the Basque country to achieve autonomy."

"I can't imagine that interests you in the least." Miguel's hand had stopped right at the edge of his jacket pocket.

"No, it doesn't," said the police commissioner. "But the life of His Majesty interests me."

"I would have thought that the old regime interested you more," said Ogoya with contempt in her voice. The tobacco seemed to have released something in Claes and Ogoya, made them get involved, while I still stood like a statue with my heart pounding and my shirt sticking to my body.

"You will never be able to understand it, *señora*," said the police commissioner with equal contempt. "You will never know what the word 'loyalty' means. At the Leader's deathbed I swore on the flag of Spain and the Holy Bible that I would serve the man the Generalissimo appointed, until my dying day. I gave him my word of honor as a soldier, *señora*. Do you understand that? No. You don't, but it's the others who are besmirching that honor. Not me. As long as His Majesty supports this ridiculous democracy, I will serve it too. Not the democracy, but His Majesty," he corrected himself.

I didn't understand a word of it; I found it bombastic, exaggerated, histrionic.

"You're a fascist at heart," said Ogoya.

The police commissioner ignored her.

"Paxti," said Miguel.

"He's mine," said the police commissioner. "He's been mine for years. Paxti is the one who turned you in."

Now Miguel's hand slid down to the pistol in his pocket, but the police commissioner kept his hands where we could see them.

"He isn't worth it," he said. "He's a coward and falls for money like a cheap whore."

"What do you want with us?" asked Miguel without expression, still with his hand in his pocket.

"I want to appeal for your help, Miguel." He was being familiar on purpose, I thought. We had to be greased, softened up. I had started thinking again.

Miguel stood there in silence.

The police commissioner leaned back against the wall.

"The king started on a tour of military installations today. He's going around appealing to the officers' conscience and reminding them of their oath of loyalty to the Leader and their sworn loyalty to His Majesty. The itinerary is secret. The overnight lodgings are secret. Only a handful of people know about them. One of that handful is the leader of the conspiracy. He is either among the leaders of this country's armed forces or at the top of the security apparatus. I can't trust anyone."

He lit another cigarette. Miguel was still standing with his hand in his right pocket. His face was impassive.

"I myself am high up in the conspiracy, but I don't know the identity of the leader. I have a suspicion, but no proof. You're probably thinking: So what *is* his role? I'm the hatchet man. I'm the executioner. I put the show on the road. I give Paxti the means to achieve the objective."

Again I could see how Miguel's body tensed. Ogoya felt it even more strongly than I did. She moved closer to him, to show him that she was with him. That she was his wife, his support. That in spite of everything the two of them belonged together. I was more moved by her small gesture than by all the words, and I felt sad, because I understood that Ogoya would never leave Miguel, no matter what other men might be able to offer.

"What does Paxti get out of it?" asked Miguel.

"Officially, a new life. He will be given amnesty when the

new regime comes to power. Plus a sum in a Swiss bank that is enough for him to support his expensive vices for the rest of his life. That's the deal."

"And the truth?"

"He'll be killed — while attempting to escape."

"Does he know what the objective is?"

"No. Only that it's some high-ranking person."

"But why is he doing it?" I blurted out.

"Ah. Señor Jensen. You're still with us," said the police commissioner. "He's doing it for money and for the chance to start a new life. Paxti learned his trade in the service of an ideology. And he's good at his job, but he is and remains a hired assassin." Once again Miguel's calm was disturbed, and once again he found strength in Ogoya's nearness.

"So what am I?" I asked. "A knight in your chess game?" Actually I had wanted to say "pawn," but all of a sudden I couldn't remember the word.

The police commissioner laughed.

"You're giving yourself too much credit. You're only a pawn. Your wife, on the other hand, was a queen, who came as if sent by the Almighty."

"What does Charlotte have to do with this?" I shouted.

"Everything and nothing," he said. It was raining harder outside, and the air in the storage room was getting thick and stuffy.

"The security in the next few days, the checkpoints on the highways, will be the tightest in years. It's already been stiff for a month. How is Paxti going to get 50 kilos of explosives transported to anywhere that's even in the *vicinity* of the king? That was almost an insoluble problem. But then, when your wife died four weeks ago . . ."

"What did you say?" I shouted, and moved forward a step, so

that I was standing between Miguel and the police commissioner. He didn't react at all, but Miguel grabbed my arm hard and pulled me off to the side.

"When your wife died four weeks ago, I saw that she could be used in two ways."

"But I just got a letter from her a few days ago."

"Paxti wrote that," he said coolly. "Luckily your wife wrote her letters on a typewriter."

"How did she die? What are you talking about?"

He continued, unfazed. "In a traffic accident on the highway between Barcelona and Zaragoza on a weekend, along with over a hundred other people who lost their lives on the road that Saturday and Sunday."

I felt like jumping at his throat. I wanted to pound and stomp that soft, fat, disgusting body to little pieces. Suddenly I was so very tired. My whole body ached; my foggy brain tried to fumble its way to an explanation, to answers to all those questions.

The police commissioner's voice continued in Spanish, which I understood better than ever before. All the forgotten words from my studies so long ago were coming back, as if they had been in storage somewhere in my subconscious just waiting for a situation like this to come up.

"I saw the report on the telex. I had publication stopped. I could use her. She turned out to be better than I had expected. Your peculiar marriage was perfect, from my standpoint at least, even if it's an unholy alliance in God's eyes."

"Get to the point," I said.

"I needed freedom of movement. I needed a smokescreen. I was involved in a plot whose success depended on my knowing as little as possible about its connections with the military and civil sectors and with the international world of finance, which were all worried about socialism in Spain. Secrecy was the alpha and omega. It's a shadow world, and I was walking a tightrope of lies. I couldn't reveal my actual reasons for movement. I put your wife in touch with international terrorism. That opens all the doors. Who wouldn't want to help in the fight against it? That gave me freedom to travel. That gave me freedom to snoop around both at home and abroad. It led me to the center of the conspiracy, and to the suspicion which now lacks only a name."

"And it blackened Charlotte's name," I said.

All I got for an answer was a twitch of his face.

He certainly knew how to set a scene. We were standing completely still. Claes had only said a single word, but he was following along attentively. I had a feeling he would be able to repeat every word we'd said. Ogoya was standing there like Miguel's shadow. Danger radiated from Miguel's eyes and tensed body — it scared me.

"When it suited me, she died," continued the police commissioner.

"And the bomb in the bar?" I asked.

"Innocent people die in every war."

"You're a murderer!"

"Technically it was Paxti's work," he said. "Morality has nothing to do with it."

"So why was she supposed to die now?" I asked without thinking how absurd the question was, without realizing that she'd already been dead a whole month.

"Because the king's travel plans are set. And because four days ago I got a call telling me that my executioner Paxti will be in a café on the road to Burgos tomorrow. He'll have the explosives with him."

He paused so he had our full attention, and then went on. "There is a sheet of paper with His Majesty's itinerary on it. Only a few of us know the contents of that paper. Only a very few people. The man Paxti is going to meet tomorrow knows the contents. He has to come in person, because in this final phase he can't trust anyone else either. He has to come out of hiding now. It's the Sardine himself who will be there tomorrow."

"Why don't you put a tail on Paxti?" asked Miguel, beating me to the question.

"Because I don't trust anyone in the security apparatus."

You could begin to understand the pressure he was under. You could see it in his bloodshot eyes, the clenched fists, and the aura of stress that seemed to surround him.

"But you trust us!" said Miguel. "That's absurd."

The police commissioner smiled again, but the atmosphere remained tense.

"It is absurd," he said. "We're natural enemies. When this is over we'll be fighting each other again. You will fight for your barbaric Basque country, I will fight for the unity of Spain. But right now we share a common interest, and no doubt you can see the advantage of our alliance."

"Perhaps," said Miguel.

"Why am I here?" I asked.

"You are a pawn, Señor Jensen. You're the chauffeur. Tomorrow you will leave San Sebastián with your wife's body. We have respect for the dead. Your wife's death is a public event. You'll be able to pass freely through the police road-blocks. Your wife's body won't be the only thing in the hearse, however. She'll be resting on 50 kilos of explosives. I'll arrange for the traffic to be diverted. Paxti will stop you and kill you. I have prepared your papers myself. Paxti has a set exactly like them. Only the picture in his passport is a little different, but men with beards all look alike, and I've arranged to run your picture in tomorrow's papers. You, or rather Paxti, can drive freely to the café and on to the objective."

I didn't know what I was supposed to say. My brain wouldn't function anymore. I had come out of my bell jar, but I was longing desperately to get back in.

Claes said, "Oh great! A car bomb like in Beirut. With the itinerary in his hand—which he will get from the Sardine—all Paxti will have to do is park the hearse under a viaduct, for example, a few minutes before the king's cortège arrives. Pretend he has a flat tire or something. He detonates it by a radio signal and . . . boom!"

I was more interested in my own affairs.

"But why me? Why the interrogation this afternoon?"

"For several reasons. I had to play my role of terrorist-hunter to the very end, you see. Maybe you were collaborating with Charlotte. I'm being watched. I needed to use you as a messenger. In addition, I wanted to see how you behave under stress. Better than I expected."

Claes ground out his cigarette with his foot, slowly and methodically. As if he were afraid of a fire, even though the floor and walls were dripping with moisture; as if the sound of the rain drumming on the roof weren't enough to remove any fear of fire.

"There's just one thing I don't understand," said Claes, immediately lighting another cigarette.

"There are lots of things you don't need to understand. You have your special role to play too."

"I'm sure of that."

The police commissioner wanted to go on, but Claes continued undeterred.

"The Sardine. The leader of the coup? You say that he contacted you earlier via secret channels, through a third party?"

The police commissioner nodded. I had a feeling of unreality again. The picture of my cozy living room and my sleeping children popped into my mind.

"Why is it necessary for him to contact Paxti directly this time? Why don't you tell Paxti what to do yourself and send him off?"

"Go on."

"I'm thinking: Maybe you know of the paper's existence but not the contents. But didn't you write it yourself? Plan the itinerary?"

"That's possible."

"But that's not the way it is?"

"No, and for two reasons. Only a few people know that I'm the head of His Majesty's secret security force. I'm not involved directly. That's the first reason. Second, through other channels I've started a rumor that reached the highest echelons today. A rumor that I am the Sardine. I'm the one they're looking for. I'm the head of the serpent."

"So then what?" asked Miguel in the silence that followed. During the pause we could clearly hear the sound of the dripping rain.

The police commissioner looked as if he were again considering whether he should go on. His double-agent life made him withhold any information he thought unnecessary to make his lackeys jump at his command. He turned my stomach.

"Yesterday the king held a meeting," he said at last. "It was top secret. I was not summoned from San Sebastián as I usually am. There were five men and His Majesty and the prime minister at that meeting. The single purpose of the meeting was to outline a new itinerary and to issue orders for my arrest. These seven men are the only ones who know where His Majesty will be during the next few days. Everyone else will find out only an hour or two beforehand."

"So your plan has succeeded," said Claes. "You're number one on the list. And who's to say that isn't really the truth?"

The police commissioner permitted himself a self-satisfied smile.

"I thought you were in the king's confidence," I said.

"I was, to a great extent. Until the evil rumors took hold." His egomania was unbearable. "I've been called to Vitoria tomorrow. I'm positive I'll be presented with the orders for my arrest."

"But then the coup can proceed," I said.

"That depends on you, my dear sirs. You are the only ones I can count on."

He was arrogant, and I hated him and his world full of blood, betrayal, and lies. He had made me a pawn, shown me in earnest that I wasn't capable of making decisions for myself. That other people had always controlled my life. I was a marionette. I guess I had always been one. Or even worse: a yes-man. And in spite of being aware of this I still didn't know whether I could walk out, pack my clothes, and go home. It bothered me that deep inside I didn't know if I was capable of shaking myself free of other people's control over every aspect of my life.

"You have a role for all of us," I said.

He looked at me with the expression of a man considering a woman's offer on the street. Does the value of the goods coincide with the price?

"Your Spanish is getting better and better," he said.

"Oh, shut up," I said, "and tell us what we're supposed to do."

15

My departure from San Sebastián was quite similar to my arrival. I drove out in a dreary morning darkness with the road shining wet. Just as when I arrived, I was not alone. It was a Seat-131 station wagon with dark tinted windows and no back seat. Behind the wire netting lay the dark-brown wooden casket with Charlotte's body resting on top of the innocent-looking explosives — or so I imagined. I hadn't looked in the coffin when I picked up the car at the commissariat. The police commissioner had handed me the papers and the key with no more formality than my signature in the presence of a notary. You couldn't read anything on his face; there was nothing to hint at the two hours the night before when he had gone over and over what was going to happen.

I'd had a hard time figuring out who I was talking to. In the morning I still had my doubts. Who was he? One minute the proper policeman — the next an instigator of torture. First the conspirator and director of hit men, then the king's faithful servant. Who was he, this man who slipped in and out of identities the way other people put on a new shirt in the morning?

We drove out of the city just before the rush-hour traffic started. There were three of us: Charlotte, myself, and Miguel, who lay covered by a blanket beside the coffin with his pistol in his jacket pocket. I was very tired after only four hours' sleep. My connection to the real world had been two phone messages from Helle, but I hadn't called her back. Claes said I'd better not. Once again I was being led around on a leash, doing what other people expected me to do.

As I drove I could sense Miguel's breathing. Although it was early in the day, I saw several patrol cars and barred Land Rovers full of policemen. After only a few kilometers there was a road-block, but they waved me right through. Had the police commissioner used his magic again and sent around the car's license number? It was an official vehicle, registered to the *guardia civil*, requested by the consul. I didn't know and didn't really care. I felt like I was wrapped in a down comforter. The black morning coffee hadn't woken me up, only made me go to the toilet several times. Miguel had been calm, with no visible signs of the lack of sleep. Ogoya had gone home with him. Claes was sitting with his finished article, waiting for the phone call that would conclude the whole thing. Or would it? What was it the police commissioner had said at the end? "Our state isn't mature enough yet for a final clash with all these powers. We'll get a breather, no more, but that's all we need." Now Claes sat waiting with his bottle and cigarettes, the police commissioner was on his way to Vitoria, and Ogoya was keeping the lines open to Madrid. The director had done his work. Now it was up to the actors.

I turned onto the *autopista* toward Bilbao, Burgos, and Madrid. The traffic was light and the car handled beautifully. It was going to happen soon. Right past the first tollgate.

There it was up ahead; I pulled into line and got my ticket. There were only a few cars this early in the morning. The countryside was unearthly in the gray light, with clouds like big cotton balls above the brownish-green mountains and small farms built on impossible slopes. Somewhere out there Paxti was waiting. Somewhere a car was on its way to a roadside café. Paxti knew the name of that café, and that's why Paxti had to disappear. Miguel and I and the police commissioner knew it too. But I didn't believe for a moment that the café was Miguel's objective. For Miguel the objective was Paxti, and the means

was the man who was waiting in the roadside café. Miguel
would meet him and keep his part of the bargain. That was what
Miguel had to pay to get near Paxti, the traitor who had betrayed
his friendship. But he would do it the way you pay off an old
debt: to get it out of the way and no longer be plagued by the
annoying collection agent.

After twenty kilometers I saw the detour sign. Dotted lines
and blockades forced the traffic into one lane and then down an
off-ramp. I stopped in back of a smoking truck reeking of diesel,
loaded with live chickens whose feathers filled the air with
snow. They didn't look like they were doing too well in the
morning cold.

A green-clad member of the *guardia civil* with a military cap
waved the truck forward. I rolled down the window and let in
the cold air. The driver of the chicken truck stuck his head out
the window and asked what was going on. The soldier said that a
tank truck had turned over farther up the *autopista*. Maybe it
was true, maybe it wasn't. The police commissioner had em-
phasized that his authority was vast. "In the fight against terrorism I have almost a free hand," he had said. "The units do
what they're told and don't ask questions."

The patrols were sent out to hunt terrorists. They didn't
know that the king was in the area — that maybe right now he
was eating breakfast before he started on his crucial tour of the
military installations near Burgos. He would show up unan-
nounced in his unmarked car to speak for the cause of democracy. He would appeal to the conscience of the officers before
they had time to prepare for the questions that he would ask
them, with all of his own authority and that of the deceased
dictator backing him up.

The soldier came over to the car. The chickens vanished in
a cloud of diesel fumes. Behind me there were already four cars
waiting. The soldier had a pistol on his belt. His partner was
standing a short distance away with a submachine gun.

"Papers, please!" he said. Oddly enough I wasn't very nervous. The papers lay beside me on the front seat, and I handed them to him along with my passport. He took a quick look at them and handed them back.

"My condolences," he said. "Have a good trip."

"Thank you," I replied to his salute, and put the car in the wrong gear so it stalled. I turned the key in the ignition, but the engine wouldn't start. I tried again and felt the sweat trickle from my armpits down to my belt before the engine caught and I got the Seat into first. We started off with a jolt, and in the rearview mirror I saw him gazing after us for a long time.

It was a narrow road. We were soon the only car on it. The other cars passed us one by one. On both sides the cliffs rose in terraces, where hay from last fall stood in haystacks that were mashed down by the weight of the winter's snow and rain. The peaks shone white whenever they weren't hidden by the clouds.

After a few kilometers there was another detour sign. The arrow pointed to the right. I turned and drove about a hundred yards, where the road curved gently around a protrusion of the cliff. When I came out of the curve I saw the white Renault van by the side of the road, just as the police commissioner had described it. The van was listing to one side with a flat left front tire. A man with a full beard stepped out in the middle of the road and waved his arms. I had no choice but to stop. Would I have stopped under any circumstances? I think so. In the confusion I would never have recognized him. But I knew who he was, and despite the full beard there was no doubt; it was the man from the embassy. It was Paxti, as they called him. I stopped right in front of the Renault. Behind me a car honked angrily and zoomed by.

I turned my head and saw him coming toward me. I thought: Miguel, are you awake? Do you know what's happening? I rolled down the window, and he leaned over. I was staring straight into the muzzle of a gun.

"Good morning, Mr. Jensen," he said in his embassy voice. "Open the door and slide over."

I did as he said, but I almost got stuck on the gearshift. And I almost made the mistake of not acting surprised. I could see the suspicion growing on his face.

"Who are you? What the hell is going on?" I said in Danish. I didn't have to pretend that I was afraid, to feign the fear in my voice, which came out hoarse and trembling. I was scared to death.

"Shut up!" he said. He opened the door all the way and crawled in sideways with his pistol pointed at me. I don't know anything about weapons, but it was a little snub-nosed revolver that looked something like one of my son's toy guns.

"Fold your hands together," he said after he was behind the wheel. He held the pistol so you couldn't see it from outside. With his left hand he fished a pair of handcuffs out of his jacket pocket. He had a blue ski jacket on, just like my own.

"Who are you?" I croaked again.

"I said shut up!" His perfect Danish sounded completely out of place in the middle of the Basque mountains, the way a Turk in Copenhagen sounds speaking to you with a singsong Fynsk accent.

"Put them on," he said. I couldn't. I clicked them onto my left wrist, but couldn't get them closed on the right.

"Give me your hands, real slow," he said. I stretched them out, and he clicked the right handcuff in place.

"Stick your hands between your thighs and cross your legs," he said. It was an uncomfortable position to sit in, but it tied me up quite effectively, and I knew that my hands would soon go to sleep. It was an efficient way to put anyone out of action.

He looked around and then put the pistol between his legs with one hand on the wheel. His other hand reached down toward the gearshift. He stiffened, and I could see why. The wire screen behind the driver's seat was covered by a loose cloth separating the front seat from the back of the car. Miguel's pistol was pressing the cloth through the wire and into Paxti's neck.

"Don't move!" said Miguel. Paxti had started to sweat, and his face was contorted in fear. I never saw anyone get so scared so fast. He was terrified, not just surprised.

"You know I want to kill you," said Miguel. "So sit real still with both hands on the wheel, tight!" Paxti squeezed his hands on the wheel.

"Take his gun, Poul." My hands shaking, I reached my manacled wrists across Paxti's thigh and grabbed the revolver.

"Sit on it," said Miguel. I shoved it under my butt.

Two cars drove by, but they only gave us a passing glance. It looked quite innocent. Two men sitting in the front seat of a car talking about an unfortunate blowout. "The only risk is a patrol car," the commissioner had said. "There is no danger unless they get suspicious or stop to ask if you need help. That's a chance we'll have to take." The police commissioner hadn't said anything about me having handcuffs on. It made the whole thing more difficult.

"Are you sitting on the gun?" asked Miguel from the darkness in the back of the car.

"Yes," I said to the police commissioner's agent, to his new assistant in this game where alliances were as volatile as love affairs.

"Hurry up!" he ordered.

I clumsily maneuvered my bound hands down into the side pocket on the door. Paxti sat rigid, with big drops of sweat on his face. He still looked scared, but he seemed to be getting over the shock. Did Miguel feel the danger growing? They had spent many years together. They knew each other inside and out. They were bound together in this dirty game. Miguel, in any case, shoved the muzzle of the pistol even harder into the back of Paxti's neck.

"Hold it!" he said. "Don't move an inch!"

"Miguel. Why?" asked Paxti.

"Shut up and don't move!"

"Sit on your hands," I said in Danish. Miguel didn't understand the words, but the extra pressure from the barrel of his gun showed that he understood the meaning.

"Slowly," said Miguel in Spanish. Paxti raised himself up and shoved his hands under him.

With difficulty I got hold of the heavy fishing line with a metal eyelet in one end and pulled it out of the side pocket. Thank God it was long enough. I wound the nylon cord under his arms just above the elbow, as Miguel had showed me the night before. I threaded the loose end through the eyelet and pulled it until Paxti's arms were trussed up like a chicken's legs and wings before you stick it in the oven.

"Pull it tight," said Miguel, and I pulled until Paxti's face grimaced in pain. But he didn't say a word.

"The gun is still pointing at you, Paxti," said Miguel. But the gun vanished and instead Miguel appeared on the passenger side, where there was no screen, only cloth. He pulled back the curtain and grabbed the nylon cord, and I could see by Paxti's face that Miguel was pulling harder and increasing the pain.

"Look and see if any cars are coming," said Miguel.

There weren't any.

"Get out!" he said. "And take the gun with you." I got the door open and wriggled out, pulling the pistol with me. It fell out into the grass, and I covered it with my foot.

"Look for the key in his pocket," said Miguel.

I leaned across the front seat and found it in his left pocket. "Watch it, Paxti!" Miguel said as I reached across Paxti's lap. His hands must have been almost numb by now. Miguel took the key, and while he held the nylon cord tight with his right hand, he unlocked my handcuffs with his left. He had wound the fishing line around his wrist and hand, which turned blue in the moment it took him to release me, he was pulling so hard.

The whole thing took only a couple of minutes. And it didn't take any longer to get Paxti into the back of the car, where we laid him on the floor in Miguel's old place beside the casket with his hands in handcuffs and his feet tied up with the nylon cord. Miguel crawled in beside him, and the last thing I saw before I drove off was the two of them staring at each other, not in hatred, but with a despair that cut through marrow and bone.

Then we took off.

"Where are you going to get rid of him?" the police commissioner had asked.

"We'll find a place," Miguel had replied.

"No, Miguel!" Ogoya had said.

"This is up to Señor Boyer," the police commissioner had decided. "I no longer have any use for Paxti."

We drove up the mountain. A few kilometers ahead Miguel told me to turn right up an unpaved road. We bumped along a few more kilometers until we couldn't go any farther. We were surrounded by pine trees. It was almost totally still. All we could hear was the sound of the drops falling from the trees. It was gray and damp everywhere. We were all the way up in the lowest layer of clouds. It was like standing in the fog.

Miguel crawled out the back and then dragged Paxti out. He fell to the ground like a sack of grain tossed down from a trap door in a barn. Neither of them said a word, but in Paxti's eyes there was unfeigned terror. Miguel pulled out a knife and cut the nylon cord, but Paxti couldn't get up on his own, and Miguel just let him lie there. A sudden fear hit me. I realized what Miguel was going to do. A horrible suspicion became reality in the midst of that dripping silence.

"No, Miguel!" I said. "Don't do it!" I don't know what came over me, but I jumped on him. I hit him with a tackle around the shoulders so he lost his balance, but he didn't fall and he didn't drop his gun. Paxti tried to crawl off, but Miguel ignored him and turned to me.

"You idiot!" was all he said. It made me furious, and I took a swing at him. I hit him on the cheek so hard that it hurt my hand, but it didn't seem to affect him much. He hit me hard in the stomach and suddenly I was sitting on the wet ground next to the car gasping for breath, as the pain shot through my gut and tears came to my eyes. I got hold of my glasses and put them on and saw two men coming out of the woods. They were about the same age as Miguel and me. They were armed with submachine guns. Miguel nodded to them and pulled Paxti upright. He hadn't made it very far.

Without a word the two men grabbed Paxti's arms and hauled him off. Paxti didn't resist, but let himself be dragged away. He only turned his head once and said, "Miguel. Try to understand."

Miguel didn't answer. He didn't even look at them as they disappeared in the dense forest. He just closed the back of the car and came over and took my arm, pulling me up. My stomach still ached.

"Are you all right?" he asked.

I nodded.

"Then drive," he said. "We've got one more meeting today."

He got into the front seat and I crawled in behind the wheel and started to turn the car around. There was no trace of the young men or Paxti. I could see his face in my mind. That look I thought he gave Miguel, pleading for help, for forgiveness. Miguel had punished him harder by his silence, his contempt, than if he had hit him. Miguel's lack of anger, lack of emotion, had been worse for Paxti than a lot of bitter, disillusioned words. Miguel was a cold bastard, I thought, and he had crushed Paxti more effectively than anyone else could have. Only in the car on the way up had there been a kind of solidarity of despair between them, but here at the end Miguel hadn't given him a thing, not even hatred. He hadn't even torn off Paxti's phony beard.

Although I knew the answer, I asked anyway, "Who were those two men?" We were bumping down the gravel road, and maybe that was why Miguel's voice shook a little.

"Two from the organization."

"You told them about the plan?"

"Of course not. I told them I had a traitor for them."

We turned onto the paved road. "You can drive right back to the *autopista*," the police commissioner had said. "The blockades will be moved. It's all right if Miguel sits in front. It's only natural that you would have a friend along."

"What are they going to do with Paxti?" I asked Miguel.

"Bring him to trial," he said. "And no doubt sentence him to death."

"What kind of trial?" I sneered as much as I could manage in Spanish.

"Their own kind. Their revolutionary court. Paxti will be executed no later than tonight," he said, as if he were telling me the score of a soccer game.

"You mean murdered."

"I mean executed. That's the punishment for treason in a war."

Then he lit a cigarette and asked if I knew the road to the rendezvous, and I tried to repress his words by wondering how the Sardine would make sure that I was Paxti. The police commissioner hadn't figured that one out. But he was sure that it had something to do with the fact that I spoke Danish.

As he had said in the dark of night, it was the only thing the real Paxti and I had in common.

16

We made it back to the *autopista* without any trouble. The blockades were gone and there was no sign of the *guardia civil* or the tank trucks. The traffic had gotten heavier. The highway sliced through the mountains in gentle curves, and I moved the hearse with Charlotte and the explosives into the left lane. We drove toward Burgos.

The police commissioner wouldn't budge an inch the night before. I had insisted that we didn't have to bring the explosives along. It wasn't necessary. They weren't going to be used, after all. But the police commissioner had been adamant. "We have to preserve all the illusions," he had said. "We have to assume that we're under constant observation. The people who are afraid of a coup will be keeping an eye on me. Maybe they will report that I'm outfitting one of the government's cars with explosives. Their superiors, who are in on the coup, will pass it on — report that I'm actually following the orders given to me. Maybe that won't happen, but we can never be sure. At the moment conflicting signals are crisscrossing all the switchboards in the government bureaucracy. The countdown has started. The flow of confusing rumors is preparing the country for a new regime."

Miguel sat silently beside me and smoked. He was staring straight ahead, but he still had that same watchful alertness about him.

"I'm surprised that you didn't search Paxti," I said. "Where is the device he was going to use for the bomb? The radio, or whatever you call it?"

"He didn't have it on him," said Miguel without turning his head.

"How do you know that?"

"Because I know him. He's a professional. With all these roadblocks it would be too dangerous to drive around with that device. He had it hidden somewhere. It wouldn't take him long to rig up the bomb."

We drove on in silence. Instead of thinking about the up-coming meeting, I was thinking about Ogoya and Ogoya's body and everything that went along with it. I thought about the fact that Miguel hadn't said a word about my relationship with Ogoya. I had the feeling that just a few hours ago we could have talked about it; but after what had happened in the mountains, I didn't know where to begin.

Miguel was the one who broke the silence.

"You're lucky, you know that?" he said, turning his head so he could look at me. I kept my eyes on the road, which cut through the mountains like a knife through butter.

"What do you mean?"

"Indirectly you owe your life to Claes. Or rather to some striking workers in Stockholm," he said in a neutral voice.

"I don't know what you mean."

"Paxti would have killed you before the two of you reached San Sebastián."

I still kept my eyes on the road, but my damn heart started pounding again.

"Can't you see it? He needed to get you through passport control, to get you registered with the police and at the hotel. But then he and the police commissioner didn't need you any-more. Your role was finished. Then Paxti could take over your identity. Paxti was a master of disguise."

I noticed that he already talked about Paxti in the past tense. Whatever was in store for Paxti, to Miguel he was a dead man.

"But that's murder of a foreign national."

"Our friend views murder as just a regrettable minor detail when it comes to protecting His Majesty." Now his voice wasn't neutral anymore; it was sarcastic.

"But Claes ruined it," I said hesitantly.

"Yes. Paxti was a good agent. He wanted to get a sense of you, get to know you before he stole your shirt. And then the two of you met Claes at the restaurant and the whole thing was ruined."

"What do you think he did then?"

"I don't know for sure, of course, but he had to get new orders. I know how he was. He was incredible in the field, but he was never any good at figuring things out for himself. A contingency plan must have been set in motion."

"And the shadow on our tail, the red Opel? Remember?"

"Of course. Another strand in the police commissioner's web. One of the other government agencies carrying out the terrorist side of his plan."

We drove for a while in silence, as I tried to grasp what he had said with my tired, alcohol-sodden brain.

At last I said, "OK, listen. Number one: The police commissioner wants to protect the king and the government of Spain. Number two: He plays along in planning a coup. Number three: He has an agent, Paxti, who is going to blow up the king. Correct?"

"Correct," laughed Miguel.

"Number four: He enters into an unholy alliance with a former Basque terrorist, a liberal journalist, and a widower because at least they don't have ties with the fascist right wing in Spain and because in this case they have interests in common with him. Is that right?"

Now Miguel laughed out loud.

"The police commissioner was right," he said.

"What do you mean?"

"Your Spanish has really gotten better in a very short time."

Offended, I kept on driving in silence, but the mood had definitely improved. After a while he offered me one of his black cigarettes, which I detest. I took one and let him light it with the car's cigarette lighter, which he held with a steady hand.

I asked him, "So how do you think Paxti would have killed me?"

"He would have undoubtedly strangled you with a nylon cord. That was his specialty. Maybe on the way to the airport," he said as if he were giving me a recipe.

His words sank in and I blacked out for a moment.

"Look out where you're going! ¡Madre!" he yelled.

The car had veered over to the right, in front of a semi that was just inches away from crushing us and 50 kilos of explosives flatter than pancakes. The truck pulled around us to the left, blaring its horn. Thank God there weren't any other cars in front of us.

"Jesus!" said Miguel. I felt relieved. It was nice to see that he could get nervous too.

"What did the police commissioner really need me for?" I asked in almost a normal voice.

"Is that number five?"

"Now listen to me — why didn't he just use Paxti?"

Miguel smiled. "I've thought about that. I think the plan was to present the world with a murderous conspiracy that was both Basque and international. Paxti was the Basque. You and Charlotte were the international branch. He worked hard at building up your identities, didn't he?"

"You're talking as if that were his actual plan."

"Take the next exit," he said, and I didn't pursue the issue, just signaled and pulled into the right lane. The weather was still tolerable; once in a while the sun sent a ray of light through the gray clouds and between the mountains, whose towering peaks loomed on the horizon. We were coming down out of them. The landscape was flattening out; there were strips of farmland and fewer trees. We paid the toll and drove out onto the regular highway, where there was much more traffic. Heavy semis plowed past with smoke trailing behind.

Miguel was keeping an eye on the kilometer stones. Then he said, "It's the next one." He was right. There was a homemade cardboard sign by the side of the road. Someone had drawn a couple of useless forks underneath a cup, plus a clumsy figure one, followed by a childishly scrawled "km." I slowed down. The palms of my hands were sweaty, and the knob on the gearshift almost slipped when I shifted down to third.

"He'll be waiting for you at the smallest, grimiest café, which is only kept afloat by the owner's extensive fence operation," the police commissioner had said in the rainy darkness last night.

It was a low building streaked with brown, with a blue corrugated tin roof. There were only two windows; there was no door, just a curtain of multicolored plastic beads. The parking lot was full of holes and there was oil on the surface of all the puddles. In one corner stood the wreck of an old Seat. Next to it was parked a newer version of the same model, almost as rusty, but it had tires and was evidently ready to roll. In front of the house was a black Mercedes that looked like it had taken a wrong turn. It was parked beside a truck full of live pigs.

We pulled in on the other side of the black Mercedes. The smell of the pigs followed us through the curtain, which rattled and clacked. Miguel had both hands in his pockets, and he had swept the whole parking lot with his gaze. He had asked me to back in so the front end of the car pointed out toward the highway, where the traffic whizzed by in a steady stream.

There were three people in the café besides the owner, who was standing behind the bar.

At the bar itself stood a man who looked like the driver of the pig truck; he was unshaven and wearing greasy overalls. He was drinking coffee with a brandy on the side, as he leafed absent-mindedly through a newspaper lying in front of him on the bar. Next to him stood a girl who didn't fit in at all. She was definitely not Spanish. She was wearing faded jeans and a red sweater with a coin-purse hanging on a string around her neck. Her mousy-brown hair was cut short, and she didn't have any makeup on. Her hands were strong and tan, and she was drinking a *café au lait*.

There were only four small beat-up tables in the café, made of cheap plastic. Filth and old paint was peeling from them. The floor was covered with cigarette butts and sugar wrappers. At least they served coffee at this godforsaken place.

At one of the small tables sat an elderly man in a charcoal-gray suit, the owner of the black Mercedes. His hair was also gray, and he was wearing rimless glasses and had the same little neatly clipped mustache I had seen adorning the lip of so many Spaniards of the upper class. He was sitting with a little glass of wine in front of him and a newspaper spread out on the table.

The owner was short and of indeterminate age. He was standing behind the bar, staring at us in amazement as we strode in and took our places at the counter.

I ordered coffee for both of us. In big glasses with milk. The girl looked up when she heard my voice. Miguel looked around. He kept his right hand in his pocket. The man in the charcoal suit turned a page. He hadn't so much as glanced at us when we came in. The pig dealer had said *buenos días* and then went back to his paper.

"You're not Spanish, are you?" the girl asked in English.

"No, I'm Danish," I answered without thinking.

"Oh wow, are you Danish?" she asked in Danish. "So am I," she added superfluously. She wasn't very old. "That's a trip. What are you doing here?"

"I'm on my way to Madrid."

"I'm on my way back home. I've been in a little village in Andalusia all winter. Now I want to go home for the spring. The springtime in Denmark is so beautiful, don't you think?"

"I certainly do."

"Are you here on vacation too?"

"You might say that."

"It's a trip that we'd run into each other here. It's not the kind of place tourists go, is it? That's what the guy over there said too. You know, the pig dealer. He said that we ought to have a cup of coffee here because he always did. He gave me a ride here this morning. Actually, I could go home by Interrail, but that sort of takes the excitement, the adventure out of it, don't you think?"

"Definitely."

"Well, I guess we've got to be going soon."

"Did you come from Madrid?"

"No, from a little town 50 kilometers from here. Believe me, I was lucky as hell. I was like staying in some little *pension* and told them I was going to France, you know? Well, then this morning José over there comes and says he's going to San Sebastián and do I want to come along? And I go, sure, you know? That was really a lucky break, don't you think?"

"It sure was."

The owner had been following our conversation carefully. Now he plunked down the big glasses of delicious-smelling coffee in front of us.

"Anything to eat, gentlemen?" he asked.

We shook our heads.

"What language is that you're speaking?" he asked in his falsetto.

"It's Danish," the girl said in Spanish, and as if she were a teacher trying to expand his vocabulary, she added, "We're Danes. We're speaking Danish."

"Ah, Danish," said the owner. "That's difficult. A very difficult language."

"Not for Danes," said the girl and laughed so you could see all her strong white teeth, obviously a product of Danish dental hygiene.

The owner laughed too.

The pig dealer finished off his brandy. He handed a couple of bills to the owner and got his change. " *¡Vamos!* " he said to the girl.

She smiled at me.

"It was really nice talking to you," she said.

"Likewise," I said, following her with my eyes as she walked out behind the pig dealer. The man with the black Mercedes was still sitting at his table, but now he folded his paper and got up. He came over to the bar to pay. He got his change and went out through the rattling curtain. We heard the pig truck start up and smelled the mixture of diesel fumes and pigs, while the Mercedes, quiet and smooth, glided out of the bumpy parking lot.

I wanted to ask Miguel what was going to happen now, but the owner was still standing close to us. He pulled out a newspaper and laid it in front of him. I felt like sitting down, but Miguel remained standing. I also had to take a piss and didn't feel like having coffee; I wanted something cold and refreshing. I was in a cold sweat and very tired and wished I were home with my kids in Copenhagen, or at least in San Sebastián with Ogoya, but suddenly I wasn't sure which I would give higher priority.

A car pulled into the parking lot. It was a beige Seat-131, the same make as our hearse, but it was a sedan. There were two people in the front seat: a younger man driving and a man of about sixty. It was hard to see through the dirty windows of the café, and he was wearing big black sunglasses. Miguel moved to the left and took up a position with his back pressed against the edge of the bar. His coffee was untouched, and he had his hands buried deep in the pockets of his ski jacket. The Seat drove slowly around the parking lot. They must have gotten word that there were two of us. That Paxti had brought along a helper. The police commissioner had thought it would be all right in the long run. They would expect Paxti to bring along some insurance. That was better than having Miguel hide. Who knows? — maybe they had their own team waiting somewhere close by, though the team would have no idea what was going on.

The Seat came closer again. Miguel had moved all the way over to the side. He cast another glance at the full bottles on the shelf behind the bar. The owner seemed nervous. He had shoved his newspaper aside and almost set it on fire with his cigarette; he was fumbling with it so much that it rolled out of the ashtray.

Miguel squinted and stared at the car, which drove up and parked alongside the hearse. The cars were the same size and almost the same color. The older man slowly took off his sunglasses and held them in front of his face for a moment. The intentional exposure was not lost on Miguel, who nodded once, twice. He recognized him. Recognized the suntanned, rugged, well-tended face on the blocky body, which would look better in a military uniform than in a civilian suit. I didn't know who it was, but he was a big name in Spain. That was obvious.

The owner was really getting nervous. And he was sweating so it ran down his face, although his café was unheated. His whole face was glistening, and two big spots were spreading in his armpits.

"Excuse me, *señores*," he said in a voice so hoarse that it almost hissed. Miguel turned halfway around and looked at him, and the certainty spread across his face. The owner retreated hurriedly and vanished through the door leading to the back room.

"Get behind the bar, down on your stomach!" yelled Miguel and hopped over the bar and down on the floor behind it. I had gotten my butt up on the bar when I felt Miguel's hand grab my jacket. He hauled me brutally down onto the floor and pulled my jacket up over my head. He opened his mouth and pressed his hands against his ears. I did the same, but the explosion still shook my eardrums so that afterwards there was almost no sound left in the world.

The shock wave blew off the tin roof, and we were drenched with liquor from the bottles falling on us. It was like being slapped around by a giant hand, but we escaped the flying glass and were spared the shock wave itself, which had blown out to the side. The outer wall and the zinc bar had acted as a protective barrier and saved our lives.

I saw Miguel get to his feet. I couldn't hear a thing. He looked dazed, but he had his pistol in his hand. I got up on my knees and tried to shake the plugs out of my ears, with no luck. My clothes, like Miguel's, were torn and shredded. I was bleeding and scraped, but nothing felt broken.

Miguel stuck his head through the doorway to the back room; the door was banging, half ripped off its hinges. He pulled his head back fast, and I saw the dust puff from the wall where the bullet hit. Someone was shooting from the back room. I couldn't hear a thing.

Miguel ran out the front door. I followed him, staggering. There was almost nothing left of the hearse. It was blown away. Only the front end remained, tipped up so the broken axle stuck straight up in the air. The other Seat had rolled several yards away and was burning fiercely. There was only one person left inside the car, the driver, and his body was engulfed in flames. The passenger lay a little ways off. Even without my glasses I could see he was missing an arm and most of his face.

I dropped to my knees and started to throw up. Out on the highway the cars were braking, presumably with screeching tires, but they didn't dare turn off into the parking lot. The café had also started to burn. The greasy black smoke blew in the wind, and out of the smoke the owner came running with a gun in his hand. His shirttail was hanging out, the blood was running down his face, and he was limping. Miguel saw him too and froze. He grabbed his gun with both hands and spread his legs like a competition marksman aiming at a target.

"Freeze!" I could see his lips shape the word. The owner turned around. I couldn't hear anything, but I saw him shoot. I had no idea where the bullet went. Miguel fired twice. Again I could barely hear the shots, but the owner's body was flung to the ground, and I could see two bloody wounds spreading across his back where the bullets had left his body.

I didn't have anything left in my stomach, so the pain ripped through me as my stomach retched one more time. Charlotte had been lying on top of the explosives, and all trace of her was gone. If there was anything left, I wasn't about to start looking for it.

I didn't have time anyway. Miguel stood there yelling at me, but I couldn't hear him. He grabbed the back of my neck and shook me like a puppy. I tried to say something, but my lips were stuck together. Then he slapped me, first on one cheek, then the other. And then once more, and I got up and followed him.

He was running with his gun in his hand. A 2CV van with a young bearded man at the wheel had stuck its nose into the parking lot. He tried in vain to get the car in gear, but Miguel was there before he managed it.

"Out!" he said, waving his pistol. "Drive!" he said to me. I still couldn't hear, but I understood what he wanted. I crawled in behind the wheel. I was familiar with the weird gear system and got it into reverse, even though pain was shooting through my whole body. The wheels sprayed gravel. Now the flames were shooting up in the air from the café. I got the van out onto the highway and we headed back toward San Sebastián.

We drove less than a kilometer before we spotted a phone booth. I braked so hard that the car almost skidded. Miguel jumped out and dashed into the booth. I saw him dial a number and wait and say a few words into the receiver, then he hung up and hid his face in his hands.

I got out of the car and walked over to him. He was crying without a sound and his body was shaking. Maybe he was crying silently, maybe I just couldn't hear it. I put my arm around him and we stood with the door of the phone booth open and held each other in a stench of smoke, blood, and liquor.

That's how we were when the patrol car found us. It came screeching up to the phone booth, and two officers got out, drawing their guns.

They approached cautiously, with their guns pointed at us. We stood there with our arms around each other waiting for them.

17

*H*elle was on the phone from Copenhagen. I could hear a little better by now.

"Where are you?" she shouted again.

"In a little Basque fishing village. I'm coming home tomorrow. How are the kids?" I asked again.

"I already told you, they're fine. They miss you. They've been asking for you. We haven't heard from you for ten days."

"I'll be home tomorrow," I said.

"Why aren't you in San Sebastián?"

"Trying to get away from all the journalists you're sending after me." I was trying to sound conciliatory.

"Damn it, Poul, it's an incredible story. You could at least cooperate."

"No way," I said, thinking about Claes, who had started the avalanche with his story, which had circled the globe via the international news bureaus. He had broken it as soon as he got the OK from the police commissioner in Vitoria.

"Are there any repercussions in Spain?" Helle asked.

"I have no idea," I answered. And that was the truth. There weren't any repercussions here in our little village, at any rate. Just a lot of talk.

"Have you done a lot on the story on the evening news?" I asked her. She was taking care of my kids, after all.

"A few segments. It's not *that* big a story, you know."

"No, I guess not."

"It probably won't be long before it happens again. There

are apparently enough people who want to stage a coup in Spain."

"Apparently," I said.

We talked a little more about the children and then hung up. Ogoya was standing naked by the window, looking out at the harbor while she smoked a cigarette. What a sight if the fishermen should happen to look up at our little hotel. She looked so beautiful in the afternoon light, which painted stripes across her body. I lay thinking about the police commissioner, who had been in Vitoria meeting with the civilian governor sent out by the government in Madrid and the Minister of Justice and the head of the king's official security force. He had explained to them how everything fit together. His proof would be a phone call with a name from Miguel. With that the plot could be nipped in the bud, he had stressed.

But was that all? Was that everything? Had the whole thing only been part of a larger scheme, of which only the outline was visible for the time being? Miguel had paid us a visit one day. He thought the bomb had been detonated by remote control. By the owner of the bar. What if all this is just the beginning? he had speculated. What if the police commissioner had planned the whole thing from the start? The bomb had been intended for the ringleader of the coup. No doubt about that. That way the government saved itself a lot of trouble. But what if the police commissioner wanted to get rid of a rival before he installed himself at the top for the real *coup d'état*? thought Miguel out loud. Franco had done the same thing when he started his revolt. This was nothing new in Spain. Miguel hadn't wanted to talk about Paxti, whose body was shown in the newspapers lying in a mountain ravine with a bullet in the back of his neck. Ogoya made it clear to me that I shouldn't pursue the matter.

One night a long time ago the police commissioner had

said, "Mr. Hylander's article is my warning shot. It says that the coup was foiled. That they can go back in their rathole again. We aren't strong enough to drive out the rats, to take up the fight against them. But we have a reprieve. Hylander's article shows them that we've caught them with their pants down."

Ogoya turned around and came over to the bed. She crawled up to me and lay down on top of me without saying a word. Here at least was something I could make sense of in this shadow world where I didn't understand very much of what was said or done. Where the alliances were transitory and ephemeral, just like my alliance with Ogoya would be.

She started to make love to me. I thought about the police commissioner's expression: They were caught with their pants down. Who was? All of us, perhaps? In any case there was no longer any doubt that today the police commissioner was the most powerful man in Spain outside the government. He had been made head of the new centralized security and intelligence apparatus. From now on, nothing in the Spanish nation would escape him. He was sitting like the spider he was in the middle of a net, watching everybody squirm. No longer could anyone question his absolute loyalty to the state after his enormous effort, for which the king had personally thanked him.

"You're not concentrating," said Ogoya, looking up at me. Then I did, and afterwards she lay on top of me and I was still up inside her.

"Will you come to Denmark and visit me?" I asked.

"Why? You can come here. Bring your kids along."

"Maybe you would feel like staying for a while."

She smiled and kissed me gently so I remembered her first fleeting kiss during the carnival.

"Or maybe you wouldn't?" I said.

"Who knows? Anything can happen."

"Nothing ever happens in my life. It's so boring and ordinary," I said, from force of habit.

About the Author

*L*eif Davidsen was born in 1950. He is a foreign correspondent and for a number of years was based in Madrid as a freelance contributor to Radio Denmark and a number of magazines. From 1978 to 1984 he was co-editor of Radio Denmark's foreign affairs program, with Spain as one of his specialties.

In April 1985 he took over as Radio Denmark's correspondent in Moscow. *The Sardine Deception* is his first work of fiction.